CW00971790

Ogre Castle

Book 1: After The Spell Wars

Robert E. Vardeman

ZUMAYA OTHERWORLDS   AUSTIN TX

2009

This book is a work of fiction. Names, characters, places and incidents are products of the author's imagination or are used fictitiously. Any resemblance to actual persons or events is purely coincidental.

OGRE CASTLE
© 2009 by Robert E. Vardeman
ISBN 978-1-934841-34-1

Cover art © Brad Foster
Cover design © Angela Waters

All rights reserved. Except for use in review, the reproduction or utilization of this work in whole or in part in any form by any electronic, mechanical or other means now known or hereafter invented, is prohibited without the written permission of the author or publisher.

"Zumaya Otherworlds" and the griffon logo are trademarks of Zumaya Publications LLC, Austin TX. Look for us online at http://www.zumayapublications.com

Library of Congress Cataloging-in-Publication Data

Vardeman, Robert E.
Ogre Castle / Robert E. Vardeman.
    p. cm. -- (After the spell wars ; bk. 1)
ISBN 978-1-934841-34-1 (alk. paper)
1. Wizards--Fiction. I. Title.
PS3572.A714O47 2009
813'.54--dc22
                                        2009004126

For Patty,

who puts up with an ogre every day

"Show me where you cast the observation spell," he ordered.

"Master, it was here. Or rather, just inside the ballroom."

Kalindi let out a gasp. Durril said, "You have nothing to fear, milady. A quick exorcism is all that's necessary."

He cast the observation spell and threw up his hands to shield his eyes. The blazing crimson burned at his face and hands. Squinting, he turned to face the center of this magical virulence.

"Kalindi!" he shouted. The hulking red form seemed to engulf the woman.

Durril cancelled the spell, and the blaze dimmed. He stood only two paces away from an ogre that topped him by the length of a long mace. Tiny eyes burned with hatred for all things living—and mortal.

Chapter 1

*The storm had built in ferocity for three days. Vio*lent hurricane winds beat into the side of the castle and made the very stone tremble in fear. Sheets of icy water hammered the shuttered windows and crept through unprotected slits to form puddles on the floor. No candle flame was safe from the wind and water oozing into the castle of Lord Northdell.

But the violent storm off the Mother Ocean did not make the young lord shake with terror. It took more. Much more.

The sandy-haired man, hardly out of his teens, swung around, sword cutting through the chilly air in his study. The blade sliced harmlessly through...something.

"Go away!" he cried. "Let me be!"

A howling not born of the wind rose to haunt him. Lord Northdell pushed away from his desk and twisted on his hard wooden chair, sword ready. He screeched in

1

abject horror when he saw the beast that had slipped into the room.

He leaped to his feet and lunged clumsily. His sword tip wobbled, and he slipped in a puddle of rainwater that had blown between the cracks in the castle wall. If his enemy had been a mortal beast, even this awkward attack would have drawn blood. It might have slain.

The beast let out a roar that shook the foundations of the castle and pounced on the prone ruler. Lord Northdell dropped his weapon and shielded his head with both arms. Tears of rage and fear formed in the corners of his eyes as he waited for the savage claws to rip the flesh from his back.

He felt only the frigid wind buffeting the walls.

He lifted his head, tears streaming unabashedly down his cheeks. His servants worked through the night, and his bride-to-be rested in her quarters in the east wing of the sprawling castle. Still, such behavior was not becoming to the heir of Zoranto the Magnificent, descendant of warriors and kings, potentates of the Plenn Archipelagos and the Mother Ocean surrounding them.

"Fight, damn you! Why can't you fight instead of running away?" He levered himself up to his elbows and peered into the gloom. A solitary red beeswax wax candle guttered on his desk. The only shadows cast were his own and the familiar ones he remembered so well from his youth. Of the ferocious creature with the curving, saliva-dripping fangs and the wicked claws capable of gutting a man he saw nothing.

But then, he never did. The ghostly monster appeared, threatened and vanished as if it had never been.

Lord Northdell knew it was here, though. The runaway beating of his heart proved its existence.

He moved away from the rainwater puddle, unsure now if it was only water—he had soiled himself on other occasions. He brushed himself off and shivered, not wanting to check for the source of the dampness.

He retrieved his sword and walked around the study. The creature had, indeed, vanished without a trace. As it always did.

He froze when he heard a baleful moaning in the corridor outside the heavily barred door. He pressed his ear against a thick oak panel and strained to understand the words.

"Freeeee meeeee!"

Lord Northdell gripped the sword hilt so tightly his knuckles turned white.

"I want to die!"

The young ruler shoved the locking bar aside and jerked open the door. Standing less than a pace from him was a hideously deformed man, his face covered with warts and open, running sores. One eye had been gouged out, leaving behind a bloody socket. A war ax protruded from the side of his head. Lord Northdell didn't bother to itemize the other injuries. There were too many.

"Go away. Leave me alone!" he pleaded.

The mutilated figure turned away and shuffled down the corridor, left leg dragging as if from intense pain. The howls of outrage again echoed through the castle.

Lord Northdell watched until the ghost reached the junction of two large hallways. It made a snappy right face and started down the intersecting corridor.

The man's mind broke. He let out a scream of fury that rivaled any spirit's. He rushed down the hall, sword cutting empty air. He skidded around the corner and saw the back of the battle-ax-embedded head. He slashed to take it off. The blade passed harmlessly through the figure. The ghost never turned to face its attacker. Death had come long ago during the Spell Wars, and it was doomed to forever roam the ways of Castle Northdell. Nothing the new lord did mattered to a phantom already eternally damned.

Lord Northdell rushed the ghost, trying to lock his arms around its body. He felt a flash of heat then stumbled and fell on his face. He looked up and saw several of his guests seated around the large dining table in the great hall. They stared at him with varying mixtures of amusement and apprehension.

He couldn't keep himself from laughing. Six of the seven at the table were living, breathing humans. The final guest was a ghost who wolfed down food from the others' plates. Each mouthful fell to an insubstantial belly and plopped onto the table or floor with just enough ghostly digestive scum on it to make it inedible.

"Lord Northdell, I must protest. This is no way to greet your betrothed!" protested an ample man at the end of the table. "My daughter is unused to such...to such..." The man sputtered for the appropriate words and failed as the voracious ghost brushed past him and dragged a sticky tongue across his plate. Wherever the vaporous tongue touched, the metal plate smoked ominously.

"Squire Denbar, my apologies." Lord Northdell couldn't take his eyes off the hungry ghost. It continued to devour anything remotely appearing to be food.

"You must understand my outrage at this, but there is nothing I can do."

"We depart for our village when the storm blows over," said Denbar. "This is no place for one so lovely as my Kalindi."

"Please, let us not be hasty, good squire," spoke up the lord's adviser. "The marriage has been arranged these thirty years. It is to everyone's benefit." The adviser cocked his head to one side and moved closer, whispering in the squire's ear. The way the fat man's eyes widened with greed told Lord Northdell that even more had been offered for his daughter's hand.

Lord Northdell had no objection to the dealing. Squire Denbar was obese and waddled. Kalindi floated like a svelte spirit. Her regular features were not displeasing to him, and the platinum-blond hair that he had at first mistaken for the purest white had been festooned with small black pearls from their village's oyster beds. Around Kalindi's slender neck dangled a strand of shining nacreous pearls and a heavier gold strand laden with brilliant red and blue stones of a variety Lord Northdell could not identify.

The young lady was a worthy match for any lord, even if the marriage had been arranged ten years before either of them had been born.

"My lord, whom do you fight?" she asked. Her voice was soft, musical and enchanting.

Lord Northdell stared at the sword he still gripped fiercely in his hand.

"I fight any who would frighten you," he said, hoping this was a gallant-sounding reply.

Kalindi sneered slightly but said nothing. Her azure eyes drifted along the messy table to where the ghost slithered like a misty snake over the upholstered seat of a chair, its long, black, sticky tongue working at crumbs clinging there.

Lord Northdell started to brandish the sword at the ghost, hoping to make it go away. He stopped before he humiliated himself.

His father had died, probably of incurable nastiness, only a month earlier and had sent word for his only surviving son to return from exile in the hills of Loke-Bor. There had never been a reconciliation between them.

The new Lord Northdell wondered if this wasn't another of his father's many vicious jokes. The castle's infestation of specters was far worse than he remembered from his childhood. A few miserable haunted souls had walked the battlements then, giving an air of mystery and chronicle to the immense pile of tumbled-down stone. He had been exiled by his father for seven years. In that time the number of apparitions had multiplied beyond all reason.

He knew the castle had been the site of many violent, bitter battles during the Spell Wars. How so many had died here, and why they had decided to remain and haunt it eluded him. A simple pass of his sword was not going to scare away any ghost in this thrice-damned castle.

He had never fully explored it since returning and had no desire to know what walked the halls after he futilely barred his doors.

Lord Northdell ducked when the ghost flung a half-filled wine goblet at him. The purple liquid streamed out, staining the table and his guests' clothing. A single drop splashed onto Kalindi's snowy white gown.

"Stop that!" he roared at the ghost. "Get out of here and leave us alone!"

The ghost looked up, as if surprised. Its huge mouth parted in an ugly grin. Then food began to disgorge from its mouth. The noxious stream spattered Lord Northdell and clung with a ferocity that defied all logic to the front of his tunic.

He went berserk again and charged the spirit, sword swinging wildly. The blade passed through the grinning head and cleaved deeply into the wood chair back. Lord Northdell lurched forward and tried to grapple the misty monster. The ghost danced away and began throwing food off the table. A new geyser regurgitated outward and splashed over the young lord.

His advisers jumped to their feet, each shouting conflicting advice. He ignored them all. He wanted blood, even if he wasn't likely to get it from a phantom. He struggled ahead, fists swinging. The ghost backpedaled and then simply vanished.

"Come here and fight!" screamed Lord Northdell. He calmed, realizing how ludicrous he appeared, not only to Squire Denbar but to Kalindi. Turning to apologize, he found himself unable to speak. Fear clogged his throat and turned his insides to ice water.

The ghost crossing the great hall carried a mace in its left hand and a morningstar in its right. Halfway to the table the massive apparition started swinging the morningstar, its chain and spiked ball whistling menacingly.

"It's only a ghost," scoffed Squire Denbar. "You're pale and shaking. I'm not sure I want my daughter marrying such a cowardly sort as you."

The spiked ball crashed into the table an arm's length away from the squire—and did not stop. The heavy ball broke through the wood and crashed into the stone floor, fat blue sparks leaping in all directions. The ghost whirled about with an agility belying its size and caught one adviser in the middle of the face with the mace. The man sank to the floor, dead from the single blow.

"It...It's real!" cried the squire. "There's substance, flesh, bone!" He yelped as the ghost snapped the morningstar back into attack position.

Lord Northdell bleated like a goat for his guards. Two halbardiers blundered into the great hall, saw the ghost, dropped their weapons and fled. The sergeant of the guard proved more stalwart. He drew his broadsword and attacked.

Metal crashed into metal, staggering the guardsman. He was a veteran of combat and spun away, keeping his balance and maintaining a position to use his heavy broadsword.

"Kill it!" cried Kalindi. "It threatened my father!"

"It's threatening us all, milady," panted the guardsman. He parried a mace blow, stepped forward and kicked at the ghostly crotch. His foot found nothing but mist. The sergeant danced back in time to have his sword yanked from his hands by the morningstar's heavy chain.

"How can it be so solid?" demanded Squire Denbar. "It's a damned ghost!"

Kalindi shrieked when the ghost reached over and gripped a handful of the snowy fabric at her throat. It yanked, exposing milky skin. A second hard tug bought forth a glimpse of even more intimate flesh. She shrieked and tried to flee. This only caused the rent in her dress to lengthen.

Lord Northdell scooped up the fallen broadsword and brought it down in a vicious arc that ended against the handle of the ghost's mace. The weapon flashed from the insubstantial hand and crashed into the far wall. It sizzled and popped and melted in seconds. The ghost roared its displeasure and turned from Kalindi, hand going for the morningstar it had momentarily tucked into its broad, metal-studded belt.

The young ruler now faced an enraged ghost wielding a swinging, flashing morningstar.

The sergeant came to his aid. The guardsman dived at the ghost's knees. He slipped through the vaporous creature but disturbed it enough to thwart its attack. The apparition turned and fled, bellowing as it went.

"Enough's enough!" cried Lord Northdell. "Sergeant, get a platoon of men here immediately. We're going after that!"

"Sire, please," the guard pleaded. "We can't kill it."

"We can drive it off. It ran from us, didn't it? It'll run even farther when a score of armed men set upon it."

Squire Denbar made weak mewling noises. Kalindi tried to comfort him as she struggled to hold together her ripped gown. The necklace of pearls, gems and gold rested in the soft vee of her breasts. Of the four others attacked, one adviser lay dead, head crushed like an eggshell under the boot of a conquering warrior. A second had been seriously injured and bled profusely. The other two had fled.

Lord Northdell ignored them—and his own fear. If he did not come to grips with the spirits haunting his father's castle, it would never be his. And it would, he vowed. He had been humiliated and reviled much of his life, by his father, by everyone in Loke-Bor. He had to show them he was capable of ruling.

"Sire, your guards," said the sergeant, his voice almost quaking with fright.

Lord Northdell sputtered. He had asked for twenty. Nine had responded.

"You will be given land and a yearly stipend for your loyalty," he said. "After the ghost!"

He raised the broadsword and tried to gesture strongly with it. The heavy blade tipped forward. He couldn't prevent it from crashing into the stone floor.

The men milled about, then summoned their flagging courage. They started after the specter that had interrupted the meal of their lord's guests.

"Lord," pleaded the sergeant, "it's going into the north wing of the castle. Let's abandon this foolish quest."

"We stop it now," Lord Northdell said through clenched teeth. He saw red because of his towering rage. The heavy broadsword turned lighter in his grip, and he pushed through the soldiers and took his place at the head of the war party.

And war it was. He'd accept nothing less against the infestation of phantasms in his castle. *His* castle.

Lord Northdell shouldered past his men, swatting at the free-floating ghosts that drifted in and out of rooms, some with open doors and others with permanently barred arches. Each step gave him new determination and courage.

"We'll get them. We will!" he cried loudly, so that the men following could hear and take heart from it.

He expected a cheer in response. When nothing came, he turned. No one followed him.

"Cravens! Fools! How dare you abandon me?"

He stormed back along the corridors he had already traversed. His anger faded and apprehension mounted. Blood smears marked the way. Some pools of blood came from under locked doors to rooms unseen since the end of the Spell Wars. Lord Northdell stopped and mewed like a small child when he saw his sergeant's fate.

The man's feet dangled knee-high above the floor. The chimerical creature holding him by the throat tossed the soldier aside when it saw the lord of the castle.

"I will eat you!" the creature roared.

Lord Northdell backed away from the ogre. When it rushed him, he swung the broadsword with a strength born of fear and desperation. The sharp blade caught the ogre just above the knee and severed heavy bone and thick muscle. Ichorous black blood gushed forth as the ogre fell, hands groping.

The stench from the monster gagged the young lord. He dropped his sword and backed away, sure that he had slain the beast. Nothing survived such a massive lost of blood. The corridors were flooded with the thick, inky fluid.

"Kill you!" the ogre bellowed, hands still clutching.

Lord Northdell watched in stark terror as the ogre rose and hopped toward him, more furious than injured. He turned and ran, not even stopping in the great hall to see how Squire Denbar and his bride-to-be fared.

He barred the door to his study and leaned against it, sweat pouring from him. For the first time in his life, he welcomed the familiar roar of the hurricane outside the castle walls. The storm was less likely to harm him than the apparitions haunting his castle.

His *father's* castle.

Chapter 2

"**I**'ll slice off your worthless ears!" Durril kicked with his right foot and squarely planted the heel on the deck, rocking forward. He lunged perfectly, the curved tip of his sharp saber taking a lock of brown hair dusted with premature gray off his opponent's temple.

"Try it and die!" Arpad Zen cried. He hesitated for a moment, his right hand brushing across the spot where he had just lost a sizable chunk of hair. He twitched the sword he held in his left hand and parried a second attempt to end his life. Durril's blade slithered past, harmlessly deflected.

Zen allowed himself a moment's thrill of success. Then he landed heavily on his back, the air blasting from his lungs. When his vision cleared, he saw Durril's sharp blade cutting small figure eights around his nose. The rolling of the ship threatened to unbalance the other swordsman and send the tip into gaping mouth or exposed eye.

"Master! Hold!"

Durril pulled his blade away from his struggling apprentice. He thrust out his hand and helped Zen to his feet. "As usual, you are technically precise but lack the spark for true fighting."

"You tricked me."

"I warned you that we fought to first blood. Do you think a foe will hesitate to kick or trip or use a hidden dagger when your attention is on the tip of his dancing sword?"

"No, master," Zen said contritely.

"You do well, but we must find some way to instill a bit of imagination in you."

"I do what I can."

Durril nodded absently, his mind already casting forth to landfall. They had sailed among the islands of the Plenn Archipelagos long enough. The time had come to nourish their emaciated purses.

"Should I continue practicing the spells?"

"You've trained enough for this day, Arpad. Go bedevil the captain and find when we put in to port. The look of yon storm tells me it is blowing past Loke-Bor. By the time we arrive, it'll be nothing more than a nasty memory."

Zen stalked off to do as he was ordered. Durril shook his head. Since acquiring the youth as an apprentice he had done his best to remove some of the boy's hidebound ways. He had failed at every turn. Zen performed complex spells but without flair. He took no joy of conjuring. In truth, Durril had yet to find *anything* Arpad Zen did with gusto. He plodded along, performing adequately but never brilliantly.

Durril shrugged it off. Nothing said an apprentice had to turn out to be brilliant, though every master wished it. If Zen learned enough to be a satisfactory wizard, Durril would have done his job as teacher. Sheathing his sword, he walked to the stern where the lookout hung in the ropes ten feet above the deck.

"What progress on the storm?" he called up.

"Master Durril, we'll miss it by a dozen leagues and a day. That's not what bothers me."

"Oh?" Durril caught the undercurrent of fear in the sailor's voice. Something worried at him. Considering they had fought their way through two different bands of buccaneers and faced down a sea serpent of prodigious proportions, the wizard wondered what bothered the crusty old salt.

"The clouds. They don't look right. Can you cast a spell to study them?"

Durril sighed. He and Zen had been granted free passage by Captain Neen in exchange for minor conjurings. Zen had been assigned the duty of rote spell casting over the food supply to prevent spoilage and maggots from devouring their meals before the crew and passengers. Durril had stayed alert the first few weeks to ward off attack from free-floating sea spirits. The Spell Wars had left magical remnants on both land and at sea.

For his part, Durril had stolen passage. He had performed a few flashy conjurations to keep the captain happy, but of significant menace he had encountered nothing.

That suited him well. He frowned as he look skyward at the clouds offending the sailor's sensibilities. Although it would amount to little, he had to make the effort.

"There, master. Those clouds. See?"

Durril turned cold inside. He took several deep breaths and forced calm upon himself. He backed off a few paces and widened his stance. Lifting hands with outstretched fingers toward a faintly pink cloud rimmed in a blue glow, he began a low chant. The surge of magic drew his apprentice. Zen knew better than to interrupt. He stood patiently, watching and waiting. Durril sensed him nearby and relaxed even more. This would be a good lesson for an apprentice.

Misty tendrils formed around the wizard's hands and grew thicker until his hands vanished. When lightning began flickering within the nimbus, he changed the chant and fell silent.

Immense bolts of energy flew from his fingers and drove into the heart of the cloud.

"Master!" cried the lookout. "It flinched! I swear by Croy's seaweed beard, the cloud jerked away as if you hurt it!"

"I did hurt it," Durril said, watching the cloud scuttle away. "Can you identify it, Arpad?"

"Free-floating," his apprentice said. "From the coloration, it must be a conjuration remnant of the master from the Isle of Wonne."

"Master Ferrako," supplied Durril.

"He's the one. The cloud floats along looking innocent, then it descends and eats the spars and mast."

"First the ropes, then the wood," agreed Durril. "You have learned well. Tell me about the counter-spell I used to drive it away."

Before Zen could speak, Captain Neen hurried up. "What's wrong? What have you found?"

The lookout began babbling. Durril silenced him with a wave of the hand. The sailor turned pale under his suntan and scurried up the rigging as if the god Croy and all his nereid daughters pursued.

Durril turned to the impatient captain.

"Your lookout has sharp eyes. He is to be commended. He sighted a remnant of the Wars once conjured by Master Ferrako that—"

"Spare me," interrupted the captain. "Are we in danger?"

"Not now," Durril said.

"Good," the captain said brusquely.

"It could have sunk us," put in Zen. "I remember seeing a similar apparition."

"And?" Captain Neen stared at him.

"And it was dangerous."

"What a way he has with the tall tale. You should teach him the fine art of embellishment," said Neen. He leaped into the rigging and went aloft himself.

"What does he mean?" asked Zen, offended. "Every time I've spoken to him he insults me."

"Face it, Arpad, you have no knack for storytelling." This was another barren field in the apprentice's farmland. Durril would keep trying to teach the young man how to till those fields but had no real hope it would sprout bright green innovative ideas.

"Loke-Bor yonder!" came the cry from aloft. Durril smiled to himself. He had grown up sailing the lanes between the tiny islands of the Plenn Archipelagos, but he always appreciated dry land under his feet. His father would not have been happy with this landlubber tendency, but then his father had been born and raised at sea. He had even learned wizardry from a sea nymph.

At this fond memory, Durril had to grin. His father had married a sea nymph, but she had died. Tiring of watery ways, only then had he turned to land and married Durril's mother.

As always when he thought of them, a touch of sadness crept into him. They had both perished during the Spell Wars, victims of a curse turned into a major spell. An entire island had exploded when a volcano was triggered magically. Chance had seen Durril and his sister Kora discussing apprenticeship with Pren'dur. He had been accepted, but his sister had not.

Durril wondered what had become of her. They had watched the island's destruction, and Kora had gone off in her grief. He had never seen her again, though he had sought her during the past seven years.

Not for the first time, his lips moved in a curse on all wizards who had fought during the Spell Wars. So much had been lost, never to be recovered. His family had perished. The Plenn Archipelagos grew new islands to replace those destroyed, and everywhere he found the Wars' remnants.

He moved his hand and sent tiny sparks flying. If he'd had it within his power, he would gladly remove all spirits, phantasms, poltergeists and other magical leftovers still haunting the islands and sea lanes.

Arpad Zen leaned against the rail beside him. "I tried to tell the captain another story. You know, the one about the sea nymph and the traveling salesman from Pin."

"The punchline didn't come out right, did it?" Durril wondered why he bothered with Arpad.

"He didn't laugh. He didn't seem to recognize it as a joke."

"Captain Neen is a busy man. Let him do his job, and soon enough we'll be ashore on Loke-Bor."

"Have you ever been here before, master?"

Durril shook his head. He had...and he hadn't. The isles of the Plenn Archipelagos blended together after a few years. How did this one differ from any of the others? He didn't know and doubted he would find anything remarkable.

"Master, look!" Zen pointed to a free-floating ghost oozing up from beneath the ship's prow.

"Harmless," Durril said, immediately classifying it. "There will be decent work for us on Loke-Bor if this ghost is any indication. They might be suffering major infestations of ectoplasmic pests."

"May I exorcise something more than a poltergeist this time? I've been practicing the spells. I know the chants and rituals."

Durril stared at his apprentice. Zen had worked hard for two years. He might lack brilliance, but he possessed a competence that would stand him in good stead when he went forth on his own, a journeyman wizard.

"We won't encounter anything major, but yes, we'll see how well you do with more important exorcisms. You've earned it—on one condition."

"Yes, master, yes. Anything!"

"Don't try telling any more jokes."

Zen's face fell. Durril laughed and slapped him on the back.

"You never know when I'm joking, do you? Go below and get our gear ready for this fine land. We'll have them lining up for our services before Captain Neen sails on the evening tide."

Durril watched the sea birds increase and saw a few ghosts fluttering among them. The birds had grown used to their ectoplasmic companions long ago and knew they did not compete for food. He tossed bits of bread from his pouch high into the air. The birds dived and sometimes collided in their haste for an easy meal.

How like humans they were. Because of this trait, Durril figured to earn decent money on Loke-Bor.

Within the hour, they rocked gently against a dock. Arpad Zen struggled with their equipment. Durril considered helping, then pushed the thought aside. A small crowd had already formed to see who had arrived on Neen's fine vessel. It wouldn't do for the master to be seen doing a menial's work.

"Gather about," Durril called, pitching his voice a half-octave lower than normal to get their attention. "In one hour, in the town's central square, we will present a raree show! Tell your mothers and brothers, tell your sisters and wives. Seldom will you see such a spectacle and never will you be offered such remarkable services."

His hands shot upward and produced a fountain of gold coins. For several seconds, the crowd simply stared. Then they fell to the dock and fought among themselves for the smallest of the coins. Durril smiled crookedly. The townspeople went off muttering about such largess. Within an hour, the gold would fade, and in two, a simple lead slug would rest in their coin purses. By that time, he would have given his raree show and attracted enough business to keep him and Zen in real gold for the next few months.

The crowd dispersed, but a single small spotted dog remained, standing with legs spread widely, almost aggressively. The dog stared at Durril, head cocked to one side. The wizard studied it. Large brown and black spots dotted the dog's dirty white sides, and one large circle ringed the left eye. Its tongue lolled as it panted to keep cool in the hot noonday sun.

As if satisfied with what it saw, the dog relaxed, then barked once and ran into the town.

"Loke-Bor is proving more interesting by the moment," Durril murmured, watching it go.

"What, master?"

"Nothing. You have arranged for transportation to the town square? I promised them a show in one hour, and I will not disappoint them. Not when money is at stake."

"You should not deceive them with the transmuting gold coins, master," chided Zen. "They will not appreciate it when they turn back into lead."

"By then they'll be amused and dazzled and will forget all about it. Trust my talents as a thespian."

Not for the first time, Durril wondered how Zen would do on his own. He lacked the theatrical bent needed to attract crowds and sway public opinion. Too many commoners still thought of wizards as the evil monsters who had fought one another during the Spell Wars. It took simple tricks, such as the fake gold coins, to lure them back and convince them of his innocence and sincerity.

A pair of dock hands helped transport their equipment to the center of town. Durril walked around the square, talking with merchants, making deals, learning names to drop into his spiel, finding out what he needed to know about Loke-Bor. By the time Zen had the stage set up with the plush velvet curtains hiding the rear, Durril was ready.

"Get them in, Arpad," he said. "And don't tell any of your stories. Just use a small summoning spell."

"Master, that isn't ethical."

"Of course, it isn't. Neither is feeling your backbone grinding against your empty belly."

Durril ducked into the enclosure behind the curtains and began changing into his stage costume. Most of his raree show depended on sleight-of-hand and simple illusion. Very few real spells were used—such magic tired him quickly, and he saw no reason to expend his powers for a quick coin or two. Better to amuse and dazzle and find patrons with *real* money.

He stiffened slightly when the hair on the back of his neck began to tingle as Zen cast the summoning spell. In only minutes, the crowd would gather. He peeked through a hole in the curtain to see the size of the audience. A familiar nervousness seized him. He forced it down. Performing always gave him a mixture of exhilaration and fear. The feeling of power over the crowd pushed away the fear and left only enthusiasm for his work. Durril pulled back the curtain and stepped onto the stage. A hush fell, and he knew he held their complete attention.

An hour later, after pulling strange animals from the air and making them vanish without a trace, doing simple mind-reading tricks and even a demonstration of how to thwart cutpurses, he made his final appeal for work. Small ghost snakes crawled up his legs; towering pillars of black threatened to topple onto him; vicious-looking phantasms snapped and snarled at those fearless souls who had pressed too close to the stage—Durril controlled them all.

At his command, the annoying poltergeists and specters popped! out of existence one-by-one.

"You wouldn't suffer a rat infestation," Durril cried. "Why put up with the annoyance of ghostly remnants from a bygone era?" He carefully avoided mentioning the Spell Wars, though he alluded to them constantly. Too many in the audience would react adversely. He wanted work, not animosity.

He clapped his hands loudly, and the last of the creeping specters vanished.

"Now for my finest trick." He spun around, his long velvet cape rising into a cone around him. He found the release on the trapdoor in the stage and touched it. A final turn and he dropped to the ground beneath, leaving only his cape on stage. The gasps from the audience told how effective it looked. Zen had released a small jet of yellow smoke at the precise instant he dropped, making it appear all the more spectacular.

Durril sat under the stage and dusted himself off, waiting for Zen to make the final pitch for work. Sitting a few yards away was the spotted dog. It stared at him, then barked and ran off, digging under the edge of the stage and disappearing into the crowd.

He crawled to the back of the stage and rolled free. With luck and the memory of the gold coins he had so lavishly dispensed on the dock, a few choice jobs might come their way.

"Master," called Zen, pushing through the curtain hiding the rear of the stage to join his master. He silently mouthed *A sucker.* Aloud he said, "A gentleman wishes to employ us."

Durril hoped that Zen hadn't taken one of the fake gold coins as deposit, as he had done before. Whether out of guilt or a misguided sense of honor or even carelessness, Durril didn't know. It had annoyed him when he had counted their take and found a stack of lead slugs.

"How may I be of service?"

The old man's head bobbed. The richness of his clothing showed him to be in the service of a lord, possibly a powerful one. The jingling of his purse told of wealth enough to keep Durril happy for months and months.

"You perform exorcisms of all types of spirits?"

"The ones I can't drink, I banish," Durril said, smiling. The old man laughed. Zen frowned. The byplay had bypassed him.

"Lord Northdell requests your presence in the castle at your earliest convenience." The old man cleared his throat. "It seems we are having a problem with ghosts."

"You've come to the right wizard," Zen said. "Master Durril is second to none when it comes to chasing away unwanted phantoms."

The look in the old man's eye almost deterred Durril. The combination of fear and pity worried him. What did this Lord Northdell really want done? It had to be more than simple exorcism.

"I'll make the arrangements, master," said Zen. He had missed the unspoken warning in the old man's attitude.

"Good. Come, youngling, we'll discuss this at length." The lord's servant hobbled away ahead of Zen, leaving Durril to wonder if simpler chores might not be available.

Chapter 3

"*They seem to be honorable men*," *said Arpad Zen,* lounging back in the fine carriage. "They brought in more than enough workers to pack our stage and other equipment."

"You're feeling cocky because you had nothing to do," said Durril.

Lord Northdell had provided everything he had agreed to—so far. Durril still waited for the knife to slide between the ribs. He had developed a healthy sense of danger when dealing with phantoms and lords. The lavish fee offered meant only lavish danger.

Still, until he saw the true problem, he had nothing to lose sitting back and enjoying the ride through the countryside.

Loke-Bor proved more scenic than he had anticipated. Gently rolling green hills rose to more significant distance-purpled peaks in the central region of the island. Crowning those interior peaks were wisps of white and occasional black, storm, clouds. The entire island had been scrubbed clean by the passage of the recent hurricane. Here and there, he saw debris from destroyed huts, and trees brought to the ground by the high wind. The commoners worked diligently to repair both their dwellings and the roads. He took that to be a good sign. Pride in citizenship indicated a ruler who dealt honestly in his contracts.

Durril snorted in disgust at the notion. An honest ruler was a contradiction. No ruler sat easy on the throne. Plots and counter-plots abounded, and court intrigue turned the best intentions sinister and evil.

The coachman drove expertly, avoiding spots in the road still not repaired and giving a smoother ride than Durril expected. He tired of the pageantry of the countryside and settled back, green eyes half-hooded as he considered everything around him. The carriage was of superb construction. That meant the lord of Northdell had wealth to back his offer of employment. With such wealth, he could hire anyone to do his exorcism. Why hire an itinerant wizard and his feckless apprentice?

"They've not seen a wizard on this isle for many months," he said aloud. "That must be it. Now, why is it they need my services?"

"The old man said the castle infestations are a recent occurrence."

"Do you want to buy a bridge from one side of the Plenn Archipelagos to the other?" asked Durril.

"There's no such thing!"

"Of course not. And there is no such thing as a recent haunting. The ghosts have been in the castle since the end of the Spell Wars. How has rich Lord Northdell lived with them ten years and is only now needing them exorcised?"

"There are tides in haunting," said Zen. "Some years the phantasms are worse. This might be a peak."

"I know that," Durril said in disgust. "There is no reason for the lord to need us in particular."

"I spoke with several merchants in the market and heard of no other wizards."

"That bothers me," said Durril. "Why not? This is a prosperous and peaceful island. I could see myself settling here and hanging out my business skull." He raised his eyelids and peered at his apprentice. "You have the skull packed properly, don't you?"

"Of course I do, master. I wouldn't lose your most valued possession."

The skull of his master proved a potent focal point for Durril's magical conjurings. With it he touched on many of the spells known by his mentor. Without it he had to rely on only his own abilities.

"Look, there's the castle. See how it spreads over the top of the entire ridge? That's the mark of a truly rich and peaceful fiefdom."

Durril had to agree, though he didn't do so out loud. His sense still nagged him that this was not what it appeared. Most people hired him to chase out poltergeists from their kitchens or free-floating sea sprites from their fishing grounds. What types of specter did a lord have roaming his battlements?

The carriage pulled to a stop just inside the thick, tall gates. Durril jumped down and hurried back to examine the main defense for the castle. The massive wood gates were in good repair. A few signs of a battering ram used against them gave mute testimony to more dangerous times. A simple spell and a quick pass of his hand caused a faint purple nimbus to rise and hover over the wood surfaces. Durril watched fleeting scenes from days and months gone.

"Master? Do you see something?"

"Nothing, Arpad. Whatever infests this castle did not gain entry by force." He heaved a deep sigh. "They want us to get rid of Spell Wars remnants again. We're up to that, I suspect."

"Master Durril?" called a young, sandy-haired man with a wild look in his eyes. Moving awkwardly and with unseemly haste, Lord Northdell rushed out to meet his exorcist. "They told me to expect you. Can you do anything about the ghosts?"

Durril looked around the mammoth courtyard. From the corner of his eye, he caught movement. He closed his eyes and muttered an observation spell. He now looked, but did not see with his eyes. Rather, he saw with a magical sense that outlined phantoms.

"Ghosts," he said softly. "Over there."

"The kitchen?" Lord Northdell seemed incredulous. "We've had trouble there but—"

Durril ignored the young ruler and walked slowly toward the door leading into the kitchen. The dancing phantasms shimmered in greens and light blues, colors indicating no real power or danger.

"There!" cried Durril. "See it?"

He intensified his spell. Lord Northdell let out a shriek of terror that chilled the soul. Outlined in bright blue mist was a headless chicken flopping about on the kitchen floor.

"A poultry-geist," Zen said, a broad smile on his lips. Lord Northdell ignored him, and the smile faded. "Do you wish me to banish it, master?"

"Do so."

Arpad Zen performed the minor exorcism spell, and the decapitated chicken vanished. The apprentice gasped when a new apparition replaced it—and this one was more dangerous.

Durril had seen the pink mist forming as the chicken's ghost vanished. He faced the large specter brandishing a large knife in its hand. A pass of his hand dissolved it, too.

"A phantom cook and his foodstuff," Durril said. "Are there more ghosts for us to remove? These are relatively insignificant and of no power."

"They're gone for good?" Lord Northdell's voice almost broke with strain. Beads of sweat rolled down his forehead and cheeks, and his blue eyes had a fevered aspect to them. Durril had seen men pushed to the edge of madness before. Lord Northdell stood only a pace from complete breakdown.

All over a few harmless ghosts in his kitchen?

Durril turned in a full circle to find more ghosts. Hints of more powerful specters lingered, but he saw nothing beyond his ability to drive away.

"The banishments will be permanent," he said positively.

The flood of relief almost caused the young lord to sink to his knees. He reached out and supported himself against a wall. "I am grateful. Whatever you require, it is yours!"

"Why haven't you employed another wizard to rid you of these...annoyances?" asked Durril.

"There aren't any others on Loke-Bor."

The wizard started to ask why then stayed his tongue. Some island inhabitants did awful things to those they considered responsible for their misery during the Wars. Loke-Bor had escaped unscathed, from the look of the countryside and the prosperity of the peasants. His reception in the town had been warm, too. Why weren't there others of his profession here?

Such a question had to be asked cautiously, with a minimum of probing. To learn the full answer without first having a hint might prove fatal.

"We can do whatever you need," stated Zen. "Master Durril is unsurpassed in his field. You might say there's no other wizard on Loke-Bor who can do better."

"He just said I'm the *only* wizard," pointed out Durril. He watched Lord Northdell's response and wondered if this was entirely true. The ruler's already pale cheeks turned a pastier white.

"What is your fee?" asked Lord Northdell.

"We'll need to roam about and acquaint ourselves with your unwanted visitors," said Durril.

"My guests have gone...Oh, you mean the ghosts. Go on. Do it. Just don't disturb my fiancée or her father. They...They're in the east wing of the castle."

"We'll not bother them more than necessary," said Durril. "We prefer to conduct the examination by ourselves rather than inconvenience you or your staff."

"Yes, yes, of course. I'll be in my study."

The young lord ran his hand through the greasy locks of his unkempt hair, licked his lips nervously and then bolted as if someone had struck him with a flaming firebrand.

"A man who knows his own needs," said Zen. "He saw right away we could do the job. I don't think he'll dicker over our price." He looked at his master. "What will we charge? There aren't many spirits about that I can detect."

"Let's explore. I'm curious about the north wing of the castle." Durril felt stirrings that troubled him. Nothing about Castle Northdell seemed right, yet he could find nothing to verify his suspicions.

Durril stopped and stared back toward the carriage standing in the center of the large courtyard. Lying under the coach was the spotted dog from town. The animal's solemn eyes followed him as he walked the width of the courtyard. When he turned back at the entry to the north wing, the dog had vanished.

"What's wrong, master?"

"Nothing." Durril got no sense of evil from the dog, but he found it curious that the animal had followed him from town. The coach ride had lasted an hour. He shrugged it off as chance. The dog might belong to the coachman and had ridden along without him seeing it.

He entered the north keep and walked slowly down the halls. Vapors and specters of all kinds floated in the air, outlined by his simple observation spell. Greens and blues predominated, revealing only minor spirits. An occasional flash of pink showed more powerful ghosts. As he proceeded, Durril banished the more robust apparitions, leaving the minor ones for Zen.

When he came to a long corridor on the third floor of the wing, he stopped.

"Master, I feel…" Zen's voice drifted off. At the far end of the hall appeared a dozen ghosts, all brandishing weapons of cloud and lightning.

"We've found a major haunting," Durril said in a normal voice. "Unless I miss my guess, these are remnants of a wizard's legion."

"All magicians?" Zen's voice shook slightly with strain.

The specters began advancing. Chains clanked, and the sound of their unearthly weapons took its toll on Zen's courage. He forced himself to stand his ground. In his youth, he had run too often. His schoolmates had called him a coward—and he had been. The power he sought through magic gave him courage, just as he brought courage to the magic.

"The weapons are magical," said Durril. "No wizard allows such to fall into the hands of riffraff. No, these were important to some magic-wielder. A bodyguard, perhaps, or even a legion of special soldiers."

"Master, shouldn't we do something? Th–There are ten of them."

"Eleven," corrected Durril. "I see why Lord Northdell felt so outclassed. Imagine awakening in the night and peering into your hall and finding them."

"What are we going to do? Which spells?" Arpad Zen backed up until he felt cold stone against his spine.

"We're going to charge the lord of this castle a princely sum for our work this day."

Durril nonchalantly ducked as the leading ghost tossed a lightning bolt at him. The sizzling, hissing spear of energy blackened the wall behind. Durril started his chants. A translucent blue vapor-wall began to rise from the floor. At first, it drifted and floated and was torn apart by drafts from under the doors along the corridor. Durril continued his incantation until it hardened into a defensive screen.

Sweat beaded his upper lip. He hardly noticed. He did the work he loved so well. A trance-state settled over him, and all he knew were the spells he cast and the approaching legion of ghosts.

Behind him, he heard Zen begin a series of his own exorcism spells. One apparition vanished. He nodded his approval of Zen's skill, slight though it was in this instance.

A fierce battle cry ripped from the ghosts' vaporous throats as they charged. One by one, they smashed into the wall of blue vapor and winked out of existence. One held back, letting the others flicker into oblivion.

"A wiser specter than the others," observed Durril.

A pass of his hand removed the protective spell wall. He stepped forward to do individual combat.

Zen moved to one side to get a better look. He cried out, "Master, your feet!"

An entire flagstone block disappeared in front of Durril. The wizard walked across the empty space as if the floor remained intact. All his concentration centered on the ghost.

"Who are you?" he asked. "At one time, you were a mighty warrior. From the evidence of your weapon, you must have served a wizard of some renown."

"Rahman'dur," groaned the ghostly warrior.

"What?" called Zen. "I didn't get that."

Durril ignored his apprentice. To become distracted now meant injury or worse. The magical sword carried by the phantom glowed a pale gold along its cutting edge. Such a potent spell could end his life in an instant. After all, this spell had endured for at least ten years without renewal—and it might have been conjured long before that.

"How did you die?" he asked the warrior.

For an answer, the specter charged. A bull-throated roar echoed along the corridor. The golden sword lifted and swung in a vicious arc that should have ended inside Durril's skull.

The wizard stepped to one side, letting the spell sword slip past harmlessly. He reached out and brushed his fingertips along the side of the ghost's face. Sparks jumped, and a crackling noise drowned out everything but the apparition's last gasp.

A gust of fetid wind blew Durril's lank black hair away from his face, and then there was nothing more in the corridor. The ghostly legions with their magical swords and throwing weapons had vanished completely.

"You did it!" cried Zen.

"Of course, I did. You expected me to expire from such a simple confrontation? Why, even this last ghost was hardly more than bright pink." Durril made another pass with his right hand and cast the observation spell again.

Tiny tendrils of blue and green poked from under the doors. Other than these minor spirits, the corridor was empty of ectoplasm. The work had been simple. *Too* simple.

"What are you going to charge Lord Northdell for this?"

"We might find other spirits about. However, it is not good business to let one so rich as Lord Northdell keep too much money. They tend to squander it on royal balls and the like. I'd prefer to squander it on things I enjoy." Durril paced the corridor, snuffing out the tendrils poking from the rooms. Each chamber he checked had been exorcised. "I think a sailing ship laden with trade goods sufficient to make us rich in Wonne is a fair price."

"So much?" marveled Zen.

"Why not? Aren't we the only wizards on Loke-Bor?"

Durril stopped and stared hard. Rocked back on its haunches, the spotted dog sat at the top of the stairs, tail wagging briskly. When the animal saw him study-ing it, it barked loudly. Then it rushed down the stairs.

Durril was slow to follow. Was this an omen—or a warning?

Chapter 4

"Too high. The price you ask is exorbitant!" The lord's adviser sat stolidly in his chair, frail arms crossed over thin chest. Every line on the old man's forehead wrinkled and rippled.

"What price can anyone place on peace of mind?" asked Durril. "The north wing of the castle is free of the remnants of the Spell Wars we found. I believe that portion of your castle had been used as a barracks?"

"How did you know?" demanded Lord Northdell. The young man's eyes grew wide. The wildness had never left him. His movements were jerky, and he started at every slight noise.

"We interrogated a ghost," Arpad Zen said, "before we exorcised it."

Durril motioned his apprentice to silence. "Another wizard outfitted those troops. They carried magical weapons still active after more than a decade."

"Rahman'dur," muttered the young lord. Durril

shot a look at Zen. They now had verification of the wizard's name given them by the ghostly warrior.

"The remainder of your castle is sure to carry traces of this Rahman'dur's handiwork," explained Durril. "The price of a clipper ship laden with trade goods adequate for sale in Wonne is a paltry one in comparison to bedevilment by all manner of specters."

Durril ducked as a poltergeist tossed a decorated ceramic chamber pot across the room. He made a few hand signs, and the playful spirit *popped!* into nothingness.

"See how easy it is for a trained wizard," said Zen. "That potty-geist had no chance at all." He started to laugh then saw that none of the others responded to his joke. He slouched in his chair, arms crossed and fists clenched in frustration.

"Give him what he asks," Lord Northdell said. "I cannot bear another instant of this haunting!"

The shrillness in the ruler's voice convinced the adviser to acquiesce to Durril's demand for an entire ship loaded with trade goods. The old man nodded briskly to indicate the deal was done.

"Have the spirits out of the castle by the end of the week," Lord Northdell said, the touch of madness fading in his bright blue eyes. "I will throw a party in celebration of my upcoming nuptials." He looked around as if someone might overhear. In a conspiratorial whisper, he asked, "The ghosts will all be gone?"

"I foresee no problem in this regard, Lord Northdell." Durril indicated that the audience had ended. The adviser left, and his young lord scuttled off toward his study looking like a hunched-over insect. Durril heard the study door slam and heavy locking-rods slide into place. A final *thunk* came when the wooden bar snugged home.

"He is still worried," said Zen. "He locks himself away like a prisoner in his own castle."

Durril didn't listen to his apprentice stating the obvious. He leaned back and stared off into space, his eyes unfocused and his magical sense strained to the utmost. Vague twinges deep down bothered him. All was not well in Castle Northdell. But what was amiss? He could not tell.

"Get out of here, you mangy creature!" Zen cursed as he threw a goblet across the room. Durril blinked in time to see the spotted dog adeptly dodge the thrown goblet and sprint from the room.

"Enough of that," he said. "You wanted to work with larger apparitions. This is your chance. Start on the west wing of the castle."

"By myself?"

"Finish by noon, and we'll both begin on the east wing. This one is going to be...interesting."

Durril experienced uneasiness. Something powerful stirred, but not enough to truly disturb him.

"You have done well these past few days," the ancient adviser said, his head bobbing as if mounted on a spring. "Lord Northdell is happier than he's been since returning to take up the duties of government."

"He's only been lord for a few weeks?" asked Zen.

"His father ruled with an iron hand. A fair man with most, but too critical of his son. He drove him away. Only his untimely death prompted the young lord to return."

"How did his father die?" asked Durril. He lounged in a chair, one leg indolently draped over the arm. He watched the guests at Lord Northdell's fancy dress ball come and go. Disdain rose when he saw some of the gaudy peacocks, but he approved of many of the women and their finery. A few had gowns woven magically. Small portions became transparent, then darkened or became foggy, giving any who watched tantalizing glimpses of bare flesh. Durril considered a small spell that would alter the cloth enchantment and turn it permanently clear. Such a commotion would amuse him for a few minutes. Certainly nothing else did now that he had eliminated most of the ghosts plaguing Castle Northdell.

The adviser and Zen continued their meaningless chatter. Then, Durril sighted a woman of surpassing beauty. He slid his leg off the arm of the chair and sat up straight. She glided into the room as if she floated rather than walked. Such grace he had seldom seen.

Hair like spun silver, piled high and dotted with dark pearls, caught his imagination. What might hide within that daring concoction? A bit of sleight of hand might impress her.

She turned, and light reflected off the strand of pearls dangling around her neck. They were worth a king's ransom, but it was the red and blue gems in a golden braid that held Durril's gaze. Deep within him stirred a sensation of power.

He rose to go meet this enchanting creature but stopped when a swarthy, stolid man motioned to her from an alcove. She lifted a feather fan to hide her expression from those dancing on the ballroom floor. Durril frowned. The look she gave the mysterious and somewhat oafish man combined disdain and attraction in a contradictory mix of emotions. She glided toward him.

He started to laugh when the peasant tried to kiss her. A mud statue had a better chance for gaining this beauty's favor. Or so he thought until he saw her throw her arms around the commoner's thick neck and draw him close. They kissed until Durril thought both would suffocate.

He strained to hear what she said. The peasant was out of place in his plain brown linen tunic and skintight forest green breeches. He did not even carry a dagger of honor, but she lavished another kiss on him in spite of this breach of etiquette. Then she pushed him deeper into shadow, and both vanished.

Before Durril took a half-dozen steps, she swung back onto the dance floor.

"Milady," he said in his best courtly manner, bowing deeply, "I have a confession to make."

"Sire? Do I know you?"

Durril looked up into her cornflower blue eyes and felt himself falling endlessly.

"I am a wizard second to none, and yet I find myself caught in a spell I cannot break."

"What might this spell be?" A tiny smile danced on her thin red lips.

"Love, milady. You have cast a spell, and even if I could, I would never break it. Your powers are too great." He held out his arm, and she took it, dainty white hand resting on his forearm.

"Do you know who I am, wizard?"

"The one who has stolen my heart," he answered.

"I am Kalindi, daughter of Squire Denbar, betrothed to Lord Northdell."

Durril hid his displeasure well. He bowed lower and took her hand. "Then dancing with the new lady of Northdell is an even greater honor."

"You are a magnificent liar." Kalindi folded her intricate feather fan and tucked it away in a broad tooled leather belt. She stepped back and caught up Durril's hand, pulling him onto the dance floor. The orchestra started a long pavane that required them to dance to each tip of a gold-inlaid pentagram on the dance floor. Durril took a few seconds to fall into the rhythm of the music, then gave his attention entirely to the lovely platinum-haired woman. She graced him with a small smile that hinted at universes he had only glimpsed before.

Every time their fingers touched, Durril felt a surge of desire for her. He tried to deny it. She was Lord Northdell's intended bride. To become involved with his employer's lover was worse than stupid. It was suicidal. The young ruler commanded a significant army and controlled all access to and from Loke-Bor.

Durril knew all this—and still the attraction for Kalindi grew.

"The fifth point at last," she said breathlessly. "I am unused to dancing for so long. In my father's village, we seldom dance more than a few minutes before resting."

"A cool breeze is blowing from the balcony. Let us enjoy it more fully," suggested Durril.

As they walked arm-in-arm from the dance floor, Zen rushed up. "Master, a moment, please. They've found poltergeists in the kitchen. They're wrecking everything."

"Then get rid of them," snapped Durril. "I place full trust in my apprentice," he said for Kalindi's benefit. "I am certain he can deal with a few remnants."

He turned cold sea-green eyes on Zen. The apprentice bowed and backed off to attend to the new infestation.

"It cannot be too great," said Kalindi. "You have done a wonderful job driving the ghosts from the castle. I heard Benso admit it."

"Your betrothed's adviser? I had never heard his name."

"How odd." Kalindi frowned, and it was gorgeous. She smiled, and it was even more beautiful. "They have kept you and your apprentice so isolated."

"The isle of Loke-Bor has little use for wizards," he said. "The lord commented there aren't any others here."

"But there are!" she protested. "At least one lives in the mountainous interior regions. Where, I do not know. He is something of a recluse and is mentioned only to frighten small children."

They leaned against the silvered railing overlooking the intricate stone battlements below. Castle Northdell had been constructed on a hillside, giving each level a different view. The north wing's ballroom dominated the third floor, affording the balconies a view of a small river flowing sluggishly toward the seaport and a heavily wooded region just outside the walls. The center of the island lay behind and out of view.

"Why do you marry him?" Durril asked suddenly.

"Is it so obvious I have no love for Lord Northdell?" Kalindi sighed softly. The moonlight danced on her hair and turned it to liquid silver. Shadows highlighted her cheekbones and turned her into an ethereal being, more lovely than any mortal woman.

"It takes no scrying spell or magical invocation to see that," he said, urging her to explain.

"Our betrothal occurred before either of us was born. Zoranto arranged it with my father to strengthen ties across Loke-Bor. My village is prosperous and has historically opposed rule from Castle Northdell."

"The wedding was more of political expediency than anything else, then?"

"I fear it was Zoranto's idea. He was a brutal, vicious man. From all I have heard, he mistreated his son grievously, even if he did well by his peasants." Kalindi sighed again and turned to face Durril. "You are so confident, so self-assured."

"Unlike Lord Northdell?"

"He is terrified by his new position. Zoranto did nothing to train him. And then there have been the problems with the...ghosts."

"They are gone."

"Not the ones haunting him. They flutter through his mind and bedevil him constantly. I have seen him slipping away mentally to a land where none may follow."

"You're calling him mad?"

Kalindi shrugged. "What is mad among the commoners is a benefit for a ruler."

Durril laughed and said, "The difference between madness and eccentricity is a fortune? Is that it?"

"Power and money, yes," she said. "Those matter a great deal."

"Your father stands to gain much from your wedding?"

Kalindi only nodded. She moved closer to Durril. His arm slipped around her trim waist. The heady fragrance of her perfumed hair caused his nostrils to dilate. He pulled her closer. Their lips brushed.

The sudden noise behind them caused Kalindi to spin away guiltily.

"Master, I'm sorry to disturb you. I–I need your guidance."

"Zen, you know the spells. Did you get rid of the kitchen sprites?"

"Poltergeists," Zen corrected mechanically. "Yes, master. But there is more. I cannot decide what it is."

Durril glanced at Kalindi. The woman touched her coiffure and gave him a significant look. He wanted nothing more than to get rid of his apprentice to explore fully what that look meant.

"What did your observation spell show?"

"I–I've never seen any spirit that glowed completely red."

"*What?*" Durril gave him his full attention now, all thoughts of dalliance with Lord Northdell's lady gone.

"Blazing crimson. So bright it hurt my eyes."

"That's not possible. I would have detected such a malignant force myself. I cast ward spells to keep out any free-floating phantoms, so nothing could have wandered in." He criticized his apprentice, but memory of the uneasiness he had felt rose to torment him. Had he missed a significant ghostly manifestation?

If he had, it could not possibly be of burning crimson intensity. Only the most malignant infestations showed red. And crimson? Durril had never encountered a remnant from the Spell Wars that showed more than hot pink.

"Show me where you cast the observation spell," he ordered.

"Master, it was here. Or rather, just inside the ballroom."

Kalindi let out a gasp. Durril said, "You have nothing to fear, milady. A quick exorcism is all that's necessary."

He cast the observation spell and threw up his hands to shield his eyes. The blazing crimson burned at his face and hands. Squinting, he turned to face the center of this magical virulence.

"Kalindi!" he shouted. The hulking red form seemed to engulf the woman.

Durril cancelled the spell, and the blaze dimmed. He stood only two paces away from an ogre that topped him by the length of a long mace. Tiny eyes burned with hatred for all things living—and mortal.

Chapter 5

The ogre towered above Durril. When it let out an ear-shattering roar, the wizard was jolted from his paralysis and acted hastily. His sword slipped smoothly from its sheath, and the tip lunged straight and true for the ogre's broad, hairy chest. The keenly honed sword-tip touched a spot just over the heart—and exploded in a cloud of molten metal.

The vibration along his sword and into his shoulder knocked Durril back. He staggered and fell heavily. He sat, staring up at the glowering ogre.

"Don't!" he called out, trying to warn Arpad Zen. It was too late. His apprentice had begun an exorcism spell.

The ogre stiffened, and let out another bellow that rocked the castle's foundations. With one hand, he lifted Kalindi high and dangled her over the balcony. A fall of sixty feet greeted her if the ogre's grip relaxed for the briefest instant.

Zen stayed his spell at the last second. He saw that dispatching the ogre meant the woman's death.

"Fight him, Kalindi," urged Durril, getting back to his feet. "Try to get free!"

The woman dared to strike the hairy brute. When the ogre tightened his grip, she let out a strangled gurgle and went limp, her life seeping away.

The ogre roared once more. This time, the magical monster pulled a long flexible rod from a belt buckled tightly around its middle. The metal whip sang and whirred toward Durril. He ducked, but the tip caught him on the shoulder. Fire blossomed and spread, driving him to his knees in pain.

Zen cast his spell, knowing full well that Kalindi might die if the ogre released her.

"Arpad, don't do it," groaned Durril. "The spell won't work. The ogre is too strong. Too well protected magically. We must use other methods to stop it."

His warning came too late. The spell engulfed the ogre and caused it to glow with a dim, pure golden light. For a few seconds, Durril hoped that his apprentice's spell *had* worked. Then the clean gold aura faded and turned an ugly red deeper than dried blood. The red darkened further, and became an inky black that formed into a single sharp spear aimed directly at Zen.

Fighting down the pain searing his shoulders, Durril rose and blocked the magical riposte with his own body. Only a fraction of a second elapsed as he cast a defensive spell that took some of the power from the ogre's magical counter-thrust. It also robbed him of consciousness when the infernal energy remaining in the black lightning exploded around him.

Durril might have been senseless for a year or only a few seconds. When he recovered, the party-goers had rushed to the balcony to see what caused such a commotion.

"It's all right, my lords and ladies," Zen said, his voice quavering. "Just a little magical demonstration. Please. Return to the ballroom and dance! Make merry! Make each other!"

A few angry mutters rose from the ranking nobles in the crowd at this crude suggestion, but they dispersed, drifting away in pairs and trios. Only Benso, the lord's chief adviser, remained. He stood with his arms crossed and his booted foot tapping.

"You should not anger the guests with your ill-conceived japes, youngling," he warned. "Such insults are grounds for dismissal from our service—and worse!"

"The worst has happened already," said Durril, struggling to stand. His legs had turned to jelly, and his guts churned like a pot of boiling lead. "Fetch Lord Northdell. Now, fool, do it now!"

The sharp command sent Benso scuttling off like some ancient, withered crab. He returned in a few minutes with his master.

"What's wrong?" Lord Northdell demanded. "This is a disgrace. You've disrupted my party, and guests tell me you and Kalindi are out here alone, no chaperone in sight." The sandy-haired young ruler sniffed the air and made a face. "What is that putrid smell? It hangs out here like a musty old cloth covering everything."

"An ogre," Durril said. He took a deep breath and recovered. His adversary's scent sharpened his wits and made him eager to pursue. First, he had to present this in the proper fashion, or Lord Northdell would sail into a black rage or turn entirely mad from the strain. "Somehow, an ogre of tremendous magical strength entered the castle tonight."

"You were hired to banish all such creatures," the lord said. His eyes took on their wild look again. Hands trembling and a tic developing below his left eye, he changed from a confident ruler into a crazed court fool.

"The ogre was not in the castle when I made my last inspection," insisted Durril.

"Wizard, you placed ward spells around Castle Northdell to prevent new ghosts from entering. You failed," said Benso, a gnarled finger wagging at Durril.

"This is no remnant of the Spell Wars. The ogre is a fully conjured creature of recent origin. You have offended a wizard, and he is sending these monsters to plague you."

"Impossible," snorted Benso.

"It's true," said Zen. "I saw the ogre. The observation spell I used showed him to stand out above all other apparitions. Even I, a mere apprentice, could not have missed such a potent presence."

"Incompetent, both of you!" raged Benso.

"Be quiet, old man," ordered the lord. He began chewing his fingernails, stumbling occasionally as he paced the length of the small balcony. "I must think. Should I abandon the castle? My father did this to me. I know it! He left me a haunted castle to bedevil me and make my life hopeless."

"There is more, and infinitely worse," said Durril. "The ogre took Kalindi."

"Kidnapped her? Impossible! No!" Lord Northdell threw himself to the floor and began ripping at his clothing. Both Zen and Benso tried to stop him. He proved too strong for them until Durril cast a mild paralysis spell on the raging lord.

"Get him to his quarters. We can talk in private there," he said. The old adviser and Zen got the lord's arms over their shoulders and carried him through the crush of the party's carefree revelers.

"Just too much of his own wine," Durril explained, smiling as if nothing were amiss.

They reached the wing with the ruler's study. Benso unlocked the door and got his master inside. The two wizards followed.

For the first time, Durril had a chance to examine Lord Northdell's inner sanctum. He was startled by what he found. The walls were stripped bare of all ornamentation. From every crevice dripped what appeared to be blood that trickled down and puddled on the cold stone floor. The table had been hacked into splinters, and the single bed's thin blanket had been shredded. Bits of food were strewn across the floor. Durril stepped carefully to avoid walking in day's-old meat and spilled gruel and gory evidence of bleeding stone.

"I always wondered how royalty lived," muttered Zen. "As lowly as it is, I prefer my life, thank you."

"My lord has not been well," Benso said, gaze darting about as if they might be overheard. "The strain of taking over from his father has worked on his nerves."

"The ghosts have done that even better," said Durril. "What do we face?"

"What do you mean? You're the expert in exorcism. You have spent almost a week prowling the corridors and getting rid of the apparitions. You, better than anyone, know what lurks in Castle Northdell." Benso's sidelong look and suspicious nature told Durril the adviser lied. The wizard reconsidered this appraisal and decided it was only partially accurate.

Benso knew much more than he revealed.

"Who is Rahman'dur, and why is he so anxious to drive your master from the castle?"

"Never heard the name before."

"Liar!" flared Durril. "The name of this wizard was on the lips of a ghost-warrior I banished the first day in the north wing. Ghosts know little—except who has animated them. Tell me of Rahman'dur and his feud with your lord."

Benso almost sobbed. "I cannot. Please, Master Durril, do not force me to tell."

"There, there," said the wizard. He put his arms around the old man's quivering shoulders. "Everything is all right in Northdell. Everything."

His voice soothed and became hypnotic. Across the room, Durril saw Zen fighting off the effects of the soporific spell. Lord Northdell already snored quietly on his pitiful pallet.

In a few minutes, Benso's head drooped and his whiskered chin touched his chest.

"What of Rahman'dur?" Durril asked quietly.

"The Valley of the Ultimate Demise. He hides there. Rahman'dur hated Zoranto. The Spell Wars. They opposed one another during the Wars."

"Was Zoranto a wizard?"

"No," came Benso's barely audible voice. "He brought in legions of them, though. Rahman'dur hated him for it. Rahman'dur wanted Loke-Bor for his own. His ambitions have never died."

"He snores too loudly to get any more information," Durril said, gently lowering the old man to the floor. "They will sleep soundly for a day and then awaken."

"What of the ogre?" asked Zen.

"The ogre means nothing. Rahman'dur is our enemy." Durril paced, hands locked behind his back. "We find the wizard, and we also find Kalindi."

"This is not our fight, master," pointed out Zen. "They hired us to rid the castle of ghosts. Have we not done this? We have no need to chase after the ogre."

"The ogre stole away a guest of Lord Northdell—from within the castle. Does that not worry you? Does it not niggle and tear at your sense of duty?"

Arpad Zen started to speak, then thought better of it. He had never seen his master in such a pique before.

"Her protection was entrusted to me. I will not let any ogre keep her!"

"What's the ogre likely to do with a mortal?" Zen asked innocently. Durril glared at him, spun and stormed from Lord Northdell's study and its foulness.

Zen followed his master to the main courtyard. Durril barked orders for horses to be prepared for them. Several of the younger stablehands hastened to obey. The rest held back, unsure what to do. They obeyed only their master, not some wizardly interloper who had spent the week meddling and poking about and making their lives miserable.

"Get a trail kit, Arpad," he said. "We're going after the ogre and get Kalindi back."

"Where did the ogre go from the balcony?" the apprentice asked. "The black lightning bolt struck you and momentarily blinded me. I saw nothing for several seconds."

"It dropped over the side. What does a fall of sixty

feet mean to a phantom with ectoplasm for bones and sinews?"

"But the girl!"

Durril waved such an inconsequential matter aside. Anyone conjuring an ogre could protect a mortal in a fall. The magics of Rahman'dur were powerful, even at a distance of several leagues. This worried him more than anything else. Vengeance sworn and extracted was common. A display of such ability foretold troubles to come. What motives lurked behind this vile crime?

By the time Zen returned with the trail kit packed with the magical implements they would require to combat Rahman'dur, Durril had mounted and waited impatiently at the main entrance. Zen swung into the saddle and stowed their gear behind him, taking his time.

"Ready, master," he said, even though his tone indicated he would rather ride for the seaport and sail for anywhere.

Durril wheeled his powerful steed around and trotted into the moonlit countryside. Zen followed more cautiously, his horse unsure of its steps along the road.

Durril reined back a half-league from the castle. He began a low chant that rose in pitch and volume until it rivaled the hunting owls' frequent screeches of victory. As the chant died, a soft purple glow rose on the ground. The misty purple flowed and took the form of giant footprints.

"There. That is the track of the ogre." He stood in his stirrups and peered into the moonlit forest. Shadows danced about, hiding everything with soft darkness. The ogre might be a few steps into the forest—or halfway to the Valley of the Ultimate Demise.

"Master, is this wise? We have no quarrel with Rahman'dur. Let's approach him as one wizard to another."

"I'll fry his eyeballs when I meet him. How dare he order his creature to kidnap Kalindi?"

Zen fell silent and rode beside his master as they followed the glowing purple footsteps through the forest. Occasional wisps of free-floating phantasms appeared. Zen motioned them away; most obeyed this simple physical demand. The few bold, stronger ones required a hurried chant and a quick spell on the apprentice's part.

By the time, they emerged from the far side of the forest it was dawn, three days had passed, and he was tottering in the saddle from exhaustion.

"Master, please, I'm unable to continue. The spells. Too many. They have worn me out."

"You should have conserved your strength," chided Durril. "We'll need every bit of power we can muster when we face Rahman'dur. I have considered carefully how he conjured the ogre. He is a wizard with few peers. Not even I could summon such a creature, much less protect it magically."

"Then, how can we defeat him?"

"There is a way. There is always a way. Remember that and you'll do well, Arpad."

"I know it was foolish of me to expend so much time and energy on the relatively harmless spirits in the forest," Zen said. "Still, ones like this bother me."

Durril let out a curse that turned the air in front of his lips a cobalt blue. He jerked hard at his horse's reins and shouted, "Flee! Run for your life!"

No matter which direction he turned, though, he faced the same inexorable marching legion of ghost warriors. He and Zen were surrounded, ringed in by magical death sent by Rahman'dur.

Chapter 6

Lord Northdell tossed and turned, his dreams filled with nightmarish creatures baring fangs and ghosts dripping cold water in his face. He tried to run. The harder he fought, the more he attracted the monsters. Moaning, crying out, thrashing—his hand hit something solid. Pain lanced all the way his arm and woke him.

"Wha...?" He sat upright on the thin pallet and stared around his pitiful study for several seconds before recognizing it. His racing heart slowly returned to a more normal rate. He wiped a forehead-full of sweat away and dried his hand on the blanket.

"Lord?"

"Benso!" The young ruler got to his feet, legs shaking and gut churning. He reached out to support himself. He recoiled as his hand pressed into ectoplasmic blood oozing from between the stones in the wall. For all their work exorcising the free-floating phantoms, the wizard and his assistant had done nothing to remove the other ghostly presences. The study was the only room in the castle where he didn't experience cold spots—and even here he had to endure the bleeding stones.

"Are you all right, my lord?"

"Yes, of course. I–I just don't seem to remember much. The wizard cast a spell on me. I know that, but not the reason for it. He hasn't turned against me, has he?"

"Lord, Kalindi has been kidnapped."

Memories flooded back when Benso spoke those words. Lord Northdell's legs gave out, and he sank to the floor, not caring his back passed through the fountains of blood geysering from the stony interstices.

"The ogre! She was stolen away from my party. How can he? How dare he!"

"You are sure it is Rahman'dur?"

"Who else? He hated my father. For all I know, he was responsible for my father's death. The ghostly infestation was tolerable, though barely. But not this. This is a...a crime!"

"The wizard and his apprentice have gone to fetch her," said Benso. "They are being paid well—too well, if you ask me—and can handle this unfortunate matter."

"No," Lord Northdell said firmly.

"Sire, please. Let those ruffians do their job. They were responsible for her safety and they failed. The ogre is a magical remnant. I know it!"

"Rahman'dur sent it to bedevil me. As ruler of Loke-Bor I cannot allow such an affront to go unpunished. If he did not bother the citizenry he would be immune from my wrath, but this is an outrage!"

Lord Northdell whipped himself into a frenzy of indignation and got to his feet, anger driving away the last vestiges of any weakness. Benso dropped to the single stool and simply watched as his liege lord ranted and raved and waved his clenched fist in the air.

"Get me an army. An entire army, dammit! I will go to the Valley of the Ultimate Demise and rescue Kalindi myself. Why wait for the wizard to do work I am sworn to perform?"

"Sire," Benso said. He fell into an uneasy quiet when he realized nothing would dissuade Lord Northdell from a war of vengeance. He took a deep breath and let it rattle out slowly. "What do you require in this army?"

"A company of pikesmen. Definitely those. They are doughty fighters. And cavalry. A company of mounted. And bowmen. I can use two companies."

"Lord Northdell, there aren't that many soldiers in all Loke-Bor. We have been at peace too long, and the cost of maintaining a standing army is—"

"Enough. I do not want to hear it. Assemble what armed and armored might you can and have them ready to march in one hour. Mind you, one hour!"

"Yes, sire."

"And, Benso, you need not accompany us. This is a quest for a young man, not an ancient adviser."

"Sire, I would feel better coming with you." The old man worried that the determination to go to Kalindi's rescue had turned Lord Northdell feverish and incapable of making lucid decisions.

"I need you here in Castle Northdell to rule in my stead. You can keep everything in good condition until I return at the head of my triumphant army. I will fly the red-and-green banner of victory! Then Kalindi will become my bride."

Benso shook his head, knowing that fantasies now ruled the ruler of Loke-Bor. To war against any wizard was a serious matter requiring months of preparation. To go against Zoranto's sworn enemy of long years took more than determination and a few armed soldiers.

Benso shuffled off, leaving his lord to plot and scheme endlessly. His loyalty was torn. As senior adviser, he ought to accompany the lord into battle, to give sage advice and prevent foolishness in tactics and strategy. On the other hand, matters in the castle required immediate and constant attention.

The old man sighed. Better to run the castle as majordomo than to perish in combat against Rahman'dur's phantom legions. He shivered as he thought of the three times Zoranto had attempted to enter the Valley of the Ultimate Demise. Each had ended in ignominious defeat. Would the young lord have the wit to return, even if he had been severely defeated, and boast of victory? Zoranto always had, and it had increased his stature among the peasants.

Benso worked with grim efficiency. Within two hours an army of more than three hundred had been mustered. In four, they marched from the castle toward their destiny in the Valley of the Ultimate Demise.

⚜

"Sire, I am concerned," said the captain of the company. "We have marched hard for four days and have not found any trace of Lady Kalindi or the ogre."

"They may have chosen a more roundabout path to the valley," said Lord Northdell, eyes burning brightly and his hands tingling with the need for combat. He had never swung a sword in anger; he liked the feelings gnawing away inside him. Righteous anger directed outward was a new emotion.

"I've sent out scouts and found nothing. None of the other roads showed travel in the past few days. One group found a band of peasants migrating from the lower slopes into the mountains."

"Why wasn't I informed immediately?"

"My scouts knew many in the party. One soldier came from their village."

"They might be spies for Rahman'dur."

"Sire," the captain said with a deep frown wrinkling his forehead, "this is not likely. By all accounts, Rahman'dur is a powerful wizard and can command the very elements. He can spy wherever he wants without using poor commoners forced to migrate summer and winter to eke out an existence."

"My father never defeated him, but my father lacked determination and my good reason. The Lady Kalindi must be freed from his grip!"

The captain scowled fiercely. These might be reasons for waging a battle, but he had tactical considerations to get approved.

"Sire, we near the entrance to the Valley of the Ultimate Demise. How do we proceed? Should I split the company into three groups? One can flank us on either side while the main body advances down the road."

"We do not split forces. To do so is folly."

"Sire, we dare not let Rahman'dur trap us. We need to be able to outflank any army he sends. Doing this will give us distance and opportunity to maneuver."

"We march straight in. He will not expect a frontal assault."

"What *will* he expect?" the captain asked sarcastically.

"Zoranto's cunning always defeated him in the end. I have no time for sly tactics or clever ploys. We march directly into the knave's lair and pluck Kalindi from his grasp."

"Fine words. I'm not sure we have enough men to do it, sire." The captain leaned forward earnestly in the saddle, both hands on the pommel. "Sire, please, attend me. We have fifty archers. The rest are swordsmen. What force can we defeat with such a mix of fighters?"

"Rahman'dur will fall. Trust me. We will crush his army."

"*His army is dead!*" shrieked the captain. "He will throw phantoms against us. How can we slay warriors who died during the Spell Wars?"

"Calm yourself, man," Lord Northdell said haughtily. "You know nothing of this fight. We will triumph. Rahman'dur cannot send an entire legion of specters against us. He lacks the power, the control, the nerve!"

"Your father—"

"Forget Zoranto," Lord Northdell said coldly.

"The men worry, sire. They exchange rumors about your ability to lead."

"It's your duty to keep them in line."

Lord Northdell rocked back in the saddle and studied the hills-turning-to-mountains around them. They were less than an hour's travel from the Valley of the Ultimate Demise. Then it would be too late to turn and run, and his men would see the wisdom of his course. He would defeat Rahman'dur and free Loke-Bor from all wizards.

Who needed them? Hadn't they ruined most of the Plenn Archipelagos during the Spell Wars? Zoranto had distrusted them even as he recruited them for his armies.

A bright flash momentarily blinded Lord

Northdell. He shielded his eyes with his hand and asked, "What causes that?"

"Sire, a scout ahead signals with a mirror. The entrance to the valley is at hand. I beg you, let me divide our forces. If one segment engages the enemy, the others can support it."

"We do not divide our force. Therein lies bad tactics."

"As you wish." The officer took out his signaling mirror and flashed instructions ahead.

"What are you saying?" demanded Lord Northdell.

"I'm recalling the scouts. We must all be in one compact unit before reaching the boundaries of Rahman'dur's territory."

"No one has been here since the end of the Spell Wars." This notion stirred the young ruler's imagination. No one had challenged Rahman'dur in all that time. In truth, much effort had been expended denying the wizard's existence.

"What is it now?" asked the lord.

The scout continued to signal, the flashes coming faster now.

"He has discovered a small band of ghostly warriors. They stand guard at the valley's mouth. We might sneak past them. There is a higher trail where we can—"

"No! We go through the entrance. Rahman'dur is not expecting that."

"Sire," the captain said in dismay, "why do you erect castle walls?"

"To keep out the enemy, of course. What a foolish question."

"Would you expect the enemy to attack a wall, or the door?"

"Both. That's why they are the best-protected parts of any well-designed fortification."

"Why shouldn't Rahman'dur expect a frontal assault to be the most logical way of attacking him?"

"We can overpower his forces. How many ghosts stand guard? A handful, you said."

"They are only the point of a very long spear aimed at our hearts, sire."

"We deflect and rush in. Simple."

Lord Northdell rose in his stirrups and motioned for the standard bearer to advance. The three hundred soldiers followed dutifully, not understanding the nature of the fight they were about to join.

The captain made a rude noise, then put the spurs to his horse and raced downhill to organize his troops the best he could. Lord Northdell might be right; he might be privy to information he was not sharing. This seemingly suicidal attack might be the only way to break Rahman'dur's power. The captain doubted it, yet did what he could to accomplish it.

They marched for twenty minutes before encountering the phantasms guarding the mouth of the Valley of the Ultimate Demise. The ghosts spiraled upward, thinning as they rose. Tiny bits of ectoplasm rained down on the troopers.

"Fire!" ordered Lord Northdell.

Archers sent flight after flight of arrows through the free-floating phantoms. A vagrant wind did more to disperse the ghosts than the arrows.

"See?" he demanded of his captain. "We have gotten past his first line of defense."

"They did nothing to us."

"My point exactly. Rahman'dur is powerless against our might." His arm rose and fell. The three hundred advanced, more confident after their victory over the guardians of the wizard's stronghold.

"Sire, there! High up!" cried the captain.

Rolling down the hillside came a tidal wave of ghostly warriors brandishing maces, swords and spears. The human archers broke ranks and fired into this insubstantial juggernaut. Within seconds, the legion of ghosts had destroyed the archers and engaged the swordsmen behind them.

"Retreat!" cried Lord Northdell. "Flee. Regroup outside the valley. Captain, get them reformed and—" He bit down hard on his lower lip when he saw a phantom, taller than the captain seated upon his horse, rear back, a heavy battle ax in one misty hand. The ax flowed, streamers of haze trailing behind it as it swung in a broad arc that lopped off the captain's head.

Lord Northdell watched in mute fascination as his captain's head tumbled along the road, the fierce scowl remaining for all time on the man's face. The body twitched and jerked, and then vanished from sight as the officer's horse bolted.

Lord Northdell let out a tiny whimper. All around him, his men were being slaughtered by warriors who did not bleed when cut and did not die when run through with cold steel. Three hundred valiant soldiers had accompanied him into the Valley of the Ultimate Demise. Within five minutes only he remained alive.

"Come and take me, you bastards!" he screeched. Madness seized him. He charged the center of the phantom army. They vanished like fog before the morning sun. Laughing crazily, Lord Northdell rode at breakneck speed deeper into the wizard's stronghold. He swung his sword at any ghost venturing too close. He could do little more than disturb their substance.

The ghosts reformed minutes after he passed, slow to resume their positions of guardianship for Rahman'dur's valley.

"Come and fight me man-to-man!" he shrieked. "Coward! You cannot face me! I have you now! You can't beat me. Never!"

Lord Northdell cried out in pain and surprise as invisible hands plucked him from his saddle and tossed him high into the air. A gust of wind caught his sword and ripped it from his straining hand. Another current sailed him into the branches of a tree. He hit one branch and doubled around the thick limb. The air knocked from his lungs, he fell to the ground and lay on his back, gasping for breath.

"You are far stupider than even your father, witless one," said the bearded, dark-haired man standing over him.

"Who...?"

Rahman'dur clapped his hands. Lord Northdell shrieked in pain as slender chains snapped around his waist. Rahman'dur bent over and fastened the links with a tiny lock.

"When you have learned wisdom, perhaps I shall return," said the wizard. He sneered and added, "Perhaps." Then he vanished into the Valley of the Ultimate Demise, leaving the lord chained magically, helpless in the hot sun.

Chapter 7

"**W**hat do we do, master?" *Arpad Zen swung around,* frantically swiveling in the saddle, looking for a break in the ring of ghost warriors marching on them.

"A spell. There's no other way," muttered Durril. "But what? We cannot hope to disperse so many specters."

Zen chanted the observation spell. None of the approaching ghosts became outlined in greens or blues. All glowed a vivid pink.

"They are of recent conjuring, not remnants of the Wars," he said.

"Rahman'dur's doing. Damn him!"

For several seconds, Durril pondered their fate. To let the legion of apparitions overtake them sealed their deaths. They were trapped, and fighting out of the deadly ring was out of the question. Even if they had an entire army at their side, the ghosts would prevail.

"Master," Zen said, the edginess in his voice demanding an answer. "What are we going to do?" He fondled the hilt of his sword, but it would not serve him very well in the next few minutes. Even if the first ghost attacking him dispersed, a dozen would take its place. Eliminate those dozen, and a hundred would follow. For as far as he could see, there were marching ghost warriors armed and looking for blood. *Their* blood.

"Dismount. The spell I must perform is too complex for us to include the horses."

"The kit? What of it?"

"I need it. Be quick now. Hurry!"

Durril dropped to the ground and began scraping away a clear spot. When he found dirt, he reached behind him and took a small candle from Zen, and placed it on his dead master's skull. The apprentice knew his job, even if he had no inkling what spell Durril worked now.

"Stand firm," ordered Durril. "We can defeat them if we become one with nature."

He began the spell, his voice low. It changed in tone and timbre, becoming the susurration of wind in the trees. He paused, added a few chemicals to the air above the candle flame then continued the chant. Sweat poured from his brow, and his hands shook with the strain of the spell.

"Master, they're almost upon us!"

"Silence!"

Durril uttered the last words of the spell and stood stock-still. The ghostly soldiers totally ringed them in

Then, they began to mill about in confusion.

"What's happening?" asked Zen.

"Be very quiet and do not move quickly. Observe and tell me what has happened."

Zen turned from side to side, then cried, "I'm a tree! You turned me into a tree!"

"Shush," Durril said, swaying to mimic a tree in the wind. "They see us as trees—and that's all. We must not break the illusion." He swayed in the other direction as a ghost swung an ax at his legs.

"He's trying to chop you down!"

"Shush, quiet, no talking."

"I'd as leaf stand here till I take root," said Zen, "if the apparitions are going to bark up the wrong tree."

Durril muttered something under his breath then stood until the ghostly army began drifting away. For an hour after the last of the ghosts had vanished, the master wizard and his apprentice endured birds and bugs and the occasional wind rustling through their illusory leaves.

"Relax, Arpad, they've gone for good," Durril finally said. "If Rahman'dur left any lookouts, they've long since drifted on. The brisk evening wind makes it difficult for an incorporeal being to stay in one place long."

"I'm exhausted," the apprentice said. "You frightened me with the spell. I had no idea what you were conjuring."

"The next time you feel the urge to make such hideous jokes, I'll try my hand at turning you into a tree permanently."

"What do we do now?" Zen shook himself as if to be certain he hadn't sprouted roots or attracted bark weevils.

"Nothing has changed. We must find Kalindi and try to get her back. The ogre's footprints have faded, and I am loath to attempt new spells to bring them out.

Rahman'dur might sense my magics unless I mask them well."

"They headed in a straight line for that valley yonder," said Zen, pointing. "Is that the Valley of the Ultimate Demise?"

"It appears too serene for such a name, but who can say? Go see if you can find our horses. I wish we'd been able to tether them before the ghost legions came."

"To have done so might have invited their death. The ghost soldiers were primed for killing."

"True. Go and fetch them—and don't use any summoning spells. Remember what I said about Rahman'dur."

"Aye, master, I'll remember." Zen rushed off to follow the horses' tracks.

Durril turned his full attention toward finding the ogre's deep footprints. For a dozen yards, he found nothing of the days-old trail, then came across a partial foot imprint that might belong to the magical creature. He placed his hand over the footprint and let the power seep into him. The tiny tingles he felt proved a beast of magical origin had passed here. Any number of other creatures might have been prowling this close to Rahman'dur's home territory. The wizard took it on faith that the powerful sensations he felt could only come from the ogre.

Seldom had he seen such a well-conjured specter. The ogre took on physical characteristics while retaining ectoplasmic ones. Durril wished he had the skill and knowledge to conjure so forcefully. His talents lay in other directions. He could disperse and drive off ghosts better than he could summon them.

He hunkered down and studied the lay of the land. Finding remnants of the Spell Wars had proven all too easy for him. Although it provided an adequate living, he wished he could have concentrated more on other realms of magic.

"Healing," he said softly. "I could have been a great healer, given the time and practice. But, no, I exorcise ghosts." He chuckled to himself. In its own way, exorcism *was* healing. He cured the dead of their unnatural affliction and contact with those still living. He aided the living in finding eternal rest for noisome spirits, sometimes of relatives and sometimes of strangers.

Loke-Bor was rife with ghostly plague. With the proper spells he had cured the island of unwanted smells and howls in the night and dripping water and other supernatural manifestations. He had already given Lord Northdell more peace of mind than the young man had experienced since assuming rule of Loke-Bor.

Durril cursed quietly when he thought of Kalindi and the effect the woman had on him. He had seen beautiful women before. He remembered others far more willing and far lovelier than Kalindi. Something about the platinum-white-haired woman spoke to his heart, and touched emotions hidden deep inside for too many years. It did not pay for a wizard to become involved romantically.

He shook his head as he remembered how his father had pined for the sea nymph he had married. No offspring had resulted, and she had died while their love still burned with the intensity of the summer sun. His father had never forgotten, and Durril thought it had affected the man's work adversely. Being a wizard for a minor lord on a tiny island at the far eastern side of the Plenn Archipelagos was no fit post for a man who could have done so much more. The volcanic explosion that had taken both his father and mother had been beyond the realm of any wizard to control, but Durril had always felt his father's power should have been honed to a higher level that might have permitted them to escape.

"Master, here are the horses," called out Zen. "I found them half a league downhill grazing in a meadow."

"Good, fine." Durril paid little attention to either Zen's story or the animals. His gaze lifted and focused on the distant valley cloaked with purple haze. "So peaceful," he said.

"It is, master. Are you sure that's our destination?"

"Can't you feel Rahman'dur's power? He is everywhere in these hills. It's almost as if he travels constantly, drifting on the wind, falling with the rains, scudding past on the clouds."

"Is that possible?"

"Of course not," Durril snapped, as angry at himself for the momentary flight of fancy as he was at his apprentice for believing any other wizard might harbor such prodigious power.

He vaulted into the saddle and urged his mount toward the distance-hazed valley. They had ridden for less than ten minutes when he signaled for a halt. He turned from side to side as if sniffing the air.

"Great power. We might be overtaking the ogre."

"How is that possible, master? He travels faster and had a head start on us."

"Off the road. Into the forest," urged Durril. "He's coming. I feel it in my gut."

"I do, too," agreed Zen. "My belly is churning and is tied into knots."

"That's just from not eating. Be silent."

Durril waited impatiently as the conviction grew that the ogre approached. Puffing and grunting and the crunch of gravel under heavy feet preceded the magical creature by several minutes.

"What are we going to do?" whispered Zen. "He doesn't have the girl with him."

"It's the same ogre. I recognize him." Durril had the creature's every detail burned into his brain. He had seen the brute for only a few seconds, but it had been enough. The vision of the ogre dangling Kalindi over the precipice had been vivid. The black bolt of lightning the ogre had bent and turned against them was even more painfully intense in his memory.

"He sees us!" warned Zen.

"He is powerful, that I'll admit," said Durril.

The ogre grunted and drew his long, slender metal whip. He stamped his feet and moved a few paces toward the stand of trees where they hid. Durril began a chant of power to give himself strength and to rob any opponent of the mettle to fight.

The ogre roared and lumbered toward them, the metal rod singing as he thrashed the air with it. Durril finished his power spell and rode out. Even mounted on his bay mare, he could not quite look the tall ogre in the eye.

"Our weapons differ, ogre, but our goal is the same. We both want the Lady Kalindi. Give her to me and go on your way in peace."

The ogre growled deep in his throat. "Rahman'dur wants me to kill you."

"Charming conversationalist, isn't he?" commented Zen.

"Back me up with a spell of weakening. Don't try to exorcise him. Remember how it turned back on us before."

Zen shivered. The black lightning had almost killed. Only his master's quick thinking and expertise had robbed it of deadly power.

The ogre bellowed a war cry and dashed forward, whip rising. Durril stood his ground, fighting to keep his horse from bucking. He finished his spell just as the ogre used its weapon.

The whip exploded in its hand, sending a molten shower of metal droplets everywhere. Most rained down on the ogre. Bits of its substance flared like tiny firecrackers. These minor wounds in its ectoplasm provoked a new round of ear-splitting bellows.

"I've hurt him, but not much. The spell driving such a creature is immensely complicated. Undoing it is no less of a task than the initial conjuring."

Durril shielded them with a masking spell as the ogre attacked. A pit opened in front of it as Arpad Zen worked this spell as well as he could. The ogre hesitated—neither master nor apprentice had expected more. The few seconds of indecision allowed Durril the time to conjure a new spell.

The ogre screamed in rage and pain and tried to claw off his left arm. Durril had worked his most effective exorcism spell on the shoulder joint. The ogre ranted and sobbed and tore at his arm until he pulled it off. He held it and stared at it stupidly, as if not realizing what he had done.

The burning eyes under the thick ridges blazed with malice. The ogre snarled and attacked them using its left arm as a bludgeon. The swinging limb caught Zen on the side of the head and knocked him from his horse. Durril dodged and finished another spell. The ogre grunted and fell to one knee.

"I should have started on its legs. The knee joints are more vulnerable than the shoulders," Durril said.

Zen shook himself and got to his feet. "Where is the girl?" he called. "Tell us, and we'll let you go."

Durril laughed. "It's not that easy. The ogre is a tight-lipped construct. Another spell will be required to loosen its tongue sufficiently for human speech such as we need."

The ogre made a strangling noise and tried to grab his own throat. A large, rough, purplish tongue unrolled and snapped in the air as the ogre asphyxiated. Durril did not let up on his magical attack. With Zen's help, they wore down the creature and would soon break the spells binding it together so well.

"Master, trouble," called Zen.

"We've got the beast well in hand," Durril said. "In a few more minutes, I might be able to get it to tell me where it took Kalindi and how to rescue her."

"Master, the legions. They're returning. Down the road. They've spotted us again."

"No, dammit, no! I will not give up this easily. We must find Kalindi."

"The wench fogs your brain, master. We can't fight the ghost legions. There are too many for us. I'm tired from this fight—and I was of no use at all before against the spectral warriors."

"I'm tiring, too. That's what makes this so necessary." Durril rushed forward and kicked the ogre, sending it flat onto the ground. "We're close! Too damned close!"

"Master!"

"Let the ogre go. Get back on your horse, and let's ride like the wind. We can outdistance them."

"They'll follow."

"They'll try. When I've rested, I'll show you a new spell, one to prevent any from tracking us. We will simply seem to vanish."

Durril swung into the saddle and glared at the fallen ogre. The creature groped to regain its arm. It shoved it hard against the gaping socket and got it in backwards. One leg refused to support it, and its tongue still lolled to one side as a result of the magical strangling Durril had performed.

"We'll meet again, old friend," Durril promised it. "The next time, you won't be so lucky."

"Master, they are upon us!"

"Then ride all the faster, Arpad!"

Durril put his spurs to his horse's flanks and raced off, the ghost army trudging after them. He didn't want to let the only source of information about Kalindi go free, but preserving his own life meant renewed opportunity later to rescue the kidnapped woman.

Still, such a retreat left a bitter taste in the wizard's mouth.

Chapter 8

"*Master, we ride into the Valley of the Ultimate De-mise.*" Arpad Zen wiped frantically at his face to get the sweat away from his eyes. The salt stung constantly and blurred his vision.

As annoying as this was, the notion of finding Rahman'dur waiting for them bothered him even more. They had barely gotten the best of the ogre—and it was but one conjuration performed by the wizard. What powers would Rahman'dur exhibit in a face-to-face bat-tle?

"Up the slope. Away from the mouth of the valley," urged Durril. The master wizard bent far forward on his horse's withers to help the animal up the steep slope. Hooves kicking and stones dancing away, they clambered to the top of a rise. Durril reined in abruptly.

"Master, what...?" Zen gasped.

Facing them were three warriors with longswords flashing in the sunlight.

"They're ghosts," Durril said, "but see how substantial they appear. The work is not the equal of the ogre's conjuration, but it is still good, very good."

"Please, do something. I–I can't remember the proper spells!"

Durril whipped out his sword and rode down on the leftmost ghostly soldier. His sword clanged noisily against the longsword and bounced upward, the tip sinking into the ghost's eye socket. To Zen's surprise, the ghost sank to the ground as any mortal might do after sustaining a fatal wound.

The wizard wheeled and attacked the slower-moving ghosts from the rear. Zen got his wits about him and started the most powerful exorcism spell he knew. Just as Durril's blade thrust home into the next ghost's exposed throat, Zen finished his spell. The remaining ghost sagged under the pressure of Zen's magics.

Durril finished the last one with a sweep that would have done little more than leave a shallow gash in a human.

"They have vulnerabilities not shared by our kind," he said. "You did well in administering the exorcism spell, Arpad. It made it easy for me to dispatch the final ghost. But remember—use a masking spell as well. We were lucky to escape detection."

"I'm shaking, master. I can't control my hands." Zen stared at them. They trembled even harder. "How am I to cast other spells when I am so out of control?"

"We've done well getting rid of them. They were worthy opponents." His voice lowered to a whisper as he added, "As is Rahman'dur. We will meet soon, but on my terms."

"Another warrior! Another comes!"

Durril turned in the saddle and saw a solitary ghost warrior lumbering toward him. The ridges around the entrance to the Valley of the Ultimate Demise were overrun with ectoplasmic guards. He sighed and cursed Rahman'dur's suspicious nature. It took skill and energy to post this many phantoms. The wizard must have worked diligently since the end of the Spell Wars to muster an army of specters this large and strong.

The ghost let out a roar and charged. Durril turned his horse to one side and cut downward with all his strength. The spectral soldier lifted his sword. The ring of steel against steel shook Durril so much it unseated him. He fell to the far side of the horse. The ghost grew in stature and bodily shoved the rearing horse out of the way so it could reach its fallen foe.

Durril heard Zen begin a masking spell followed by another exorcism spell. The effect on this powerful ghost was minimal.

Durril looked up into death. The ghost's eyes had been cut out, leaving only hollow sockets. The side of its pink, vaporous face had been sliced away to expose misty bone and unbleeding putrescent flesh. The mouth opened in another roar and exposed two rows of yellowed, broken teeth.

The thick neck corded with phantom muscles and the shoulders knotted as the sword came up for the killing blow. Durril feinted to the left and rolled right. Part of his tunic was sliced away as the ghost missed with its deadly stroke.

Slow in recovering, the ghost stared at the ground as if it couldn't believe it had missed. Durril came to his feet easily and thrust. His blade cut into the giant ghost's upper arm. Mist exploded as if under pressure. The specter turned empty eye sockets toward Durril and let out another bellow, this time of rage and even pain. The leak in its upper arm widened, and the entire ghost deflated until only thin fog wound around the wizard's ankles.

"Master, how did you do that? I've never seen such a spell!"

"I didn't realize it was possible, either," he said. "I had no time for the full exorcism spell." Durril held up his sword and examined the tip. It might have been dipped in fresh blood. The cutting edge and the sharp end dripped. "This is an interesting side effect of the spell. I gave the steel a minor spell to enhance its cutting power. I had no idea it would work against the fabric of the ghost."

The master wizard went off muttering to himself. Zen followed, leading the horses.

"We rest for a time," declared Durril. "I must record my discovery. A simple edge enhancement spell can be used to dissipate ghostly ectoplasm. How unusual."

"You can present this at the next Grand Conclave," suggested Zen. "The others will be interested to learn of this."

"Tell those fools? Have them steal my innovation? Never! My grimoire. Hand me the grimoire so that I may properly record this." Durril took the small spell book and the enchanted pen he used to record his most secret thoughts and incantations and began outlining the anti-ghost procedure.

An hour later, he sighed, closed the grimoire and handed it back to Zen. The apprentice yearned to open the book and read all that his master had entered over the years, but he knew it wasn't possible. Spells protected the book, making it impossible for anyone to read without Durril's permission.

Zen smiled wryly. When he had been with Durril for less than a month, he had attempted to discover the secret of a complex weather avoidance spell by reading the book. He had gone blind for two days, and Durril had been adamant in letting the protective spell wear off rather than returning sight to him immediately. Zen had never forgotten that lesson. Meddling with another wizard's grimoire was serious business.

"You know the spell I used?" spoke up Durril.

"The edge-enhancement spell? Yes, master."

"Then use your head. Get your own grimoire out and write this down. Just because I discovered its usefulness against ghosts doesn't mean you can't use it, too. You are my apprentice and are supposed to learn. So learn, dammit!"

Zen hurriedly scribbled his own notes into a volume bound in unborn-calf leather. Although it was not protected with elaborate spells, he had devised a small one of his own to prevent non-wizards from peeking in. It would not work against any who had been admitted to the Grand Conclave, but if a peasant happened across the book, it would prevent the curious from creating havoc.

"I sense ghosts all around us," said Durril. "I hesitate to use an observation spell because of Rahman'dur."

"If they find us, will they all try to kill us?"

"Something has aroused them," said Durril. "I don't get the sensation of normal activity."

"What could it be? Has Rahman'dur alerted them because of Kalindi's kidnaping?"

Durril shook his head tiredly. He had conjured well and often, and it had taken much out of him. He leaned against a tree, head dipping until his chin touched his chest. In a sleepy voice he told his apprentice, "That is possible. There is something more causing the ruckus, however. Stand guard and wake me if the need arises."

Within a few seconds, Durril slept. His dreams came quickly—dreams of torture and madness and being crushed by incredible falling weights. He stirred and moaned softly, not quite awakening. Visions of a huge underground city filled his nightmare. The lacy, towering spires possessed great beauty, and from these he took power. The evil backed away, and he rested more fully until Zen shook him.

"What's wrong?" he demanded. "I was exploring in my dreams."

"Where, master?"

"I'm not sure, but it must be close. I never have such intense visions unless the subject is at hand." Durril shook the last vestiges of sleep off and asked, "Why did you awaken me?"

"There. Something is moving, and my observation spell will not give me a clear picture."

Durril muttered a spell of his own, then shook his head. "You've become too narrow in your thinking, Arpad. Why do you think an observation spell to reveal ghosts would not work?"

"More potent magics hide it?" answered the apprentice.

"Possibly. A better reason is at hand. Look. A mere mortal. Does he have any appearance of a ghost about him?" Durril pointed to a hunched-over old man with a beard that dangled almost to his knees. The wind shifted direction, and both men's noses wrinkled in response to pungent body odor. This old man and soap were strangers.

"Poltergeists often produce such a stench," Zen said, unsure of himself.

"Not even a ghost would tolerate such filth," said Durril. He narrowed his eyes as he studied the old man more closely. The satchel he dragged was partially open. Sunlight glinted off bright metal—metal such as that used in armor and swords.

Durril got to his feet and carefully surveyed the terrain. His observation spell revealed no ghosts. With a bold step, he quickly caught up with the tattered old man.

"Good day to you, sir."

The man jumped as if stuck by a pin.

"What do you want? Who are you? Get away!"

"I'm fine, thank you," Durril went on, as if conducting a polite conversation. "We have become lost in these hills. Can you direct us?"

"Danger lies everywhere. Deadly. Very dangerous," the old man babbled. "Go away quickly, or he'll kill you!"

"Are you referring to Rahman'dur?"

"You know him? And still you stay? Fools! You're both fools of the first water!"

Durril's observation of the man intensified. The shabby clothing and stench were not mere camouflage; they were permanent attributes. The flies landing on the man's face remained there. Bugs of indeterminate size and species crawled through his clothing, poking their antennae from rents before burrowing back in to find their nests.

"Rahman'dur is a wizard, as I am. We have much in common, the two of us."

"No!" The denial was vehement. The old man backed away another step. His eyes darted toward the satchel and back to Durril, as if the newcomer might try to steal his booty.

"How did you come by such fine armor?" asked Arpad Zen, circling around to get a better look into the canvas bag.

The old man dived and threw his scrawny body over the prize. "It's all mine. I stole it fairly!"

"I'm sure," Durril said dryly. "But do I detect the crest of the Lord Northdell on that sword?"

"Perhaps," the old man said, his arms clutching the bag tightly to his body. "What's it to you? You're a wizard. You said so."

"A wizard in Lord Northdell's employ," said Zen. "It would benefit you greatly to give answers to our questions. Where did you get the weapons and armor in the satchel?"

The old man started to lie. Zen cast a small truth spell. The man's mouth worked like the lips of a fish out of water. He croaked twice then gasped out, "I stole them off the bodies."

"The corpses of Lord Northdell's troops?" asked Durril, surprised. "Are they near?"

"The fools rode into the Valley of the Ultimate Demise. No one leaves—unless Rahman'dur permits it."

"Yet you say you robbed them like a ghoul. How is it *you* left the valley? Are you in league with Rahman'dur?" Arpad cocked his head to one side, trying to piece this puzzle together.

"No, he doesn't even know I exist. I'm a dung beetle scuttling about taking what no one else wants. He leaves me be because he doesn't ever see me."

"The valley is guarded by potent ward spells," pointed out Durril. "How do you get in and out unless Rahman'dur permits it?"

The old man cackled demoniacally. "I'm the clever one, I am, I am." He cackled again and pulled his satchel even closer.

Durril wondered if the old man might hurt himself on the exposed blade in the bag.

"We're sure of that," Zen said, his nose beginning to drip. Such proximity to the old man caused a nasal reaction. "Tell us of Lord Northdell's men. How did they come to be...dead?"

"Rahman'dur killed them, one and all, he did," the shabby man crowed. "I sat on the hillside and watched them march down into the valley mouth as bold as brass. No one leaves the Valley of the Ultimate Demise. No one, and certainly not fools like them."

"Tell us more," urged Durril. He squatted down and waited. He had to reinforce Zen's spell to keep the old man talking.

"A full three hundred guardsmen marched into the valley, never to return. Archers filled the sky with arrows. Swordsmen slashed and hacked and fought bravely—but who can win against thrice-damned ghost legions? Rahman'dur sent his best, he did, and they overpowered Lord Northdell."

"Was the lord with them?"

"He led them to their deaths! Never have I seen such a witling. They dropped behind him, brave and foolish. And he charged! He raced on into the Valley of the Ultimate Demise, and Rahman'dur's nasty specters wiped out his army to the last man. To the last one, yes, yes. It was no fit battle-death for them, no."

Durril and Zen exchanged hard glances. "What of the lord?" asked the wizard. "How did he die?"

"Die? He was too stupid to die. He didn't even know he was *supposed* to die! Rahman'dur has him chained out in the hot sun for all to see. Every ghost that drifts by reviles Lord Northdell. And he deserves it! What a fool!"

"Your truth spell is working too well," said Arpad Zen. "He not only tells us what happened, he passes judgment."

"Deservedly so, if what he says is even close to the truth. Why did Lord Northdell choose to launch a frontal attack against Rahman'dur? A wizard cannot be taken that way."

"Our employer has sheep grazing here," Zen said, tapping the side of his head. "Who can say what he'll bleat?"

"He'll last many a day before he dies, mark my words," the scavenger said. "Rahman'dur toys with his victims before he lets them die. Now and again he must let his ghost legions do some work to stay alert—that's why he let them vanquish the lord's army. But Lord Northdell? He'll last a month or more!"

"He's safe for the time being," said Durril. "We still don't know where Rahman'dur has Kalindi hidden away."

He closed his eyes and let the image of the vast city of lacy spires and glowing cut crystals return in his mind. Such a dream had something to do with Kalindi; Durril could not gainsay his own powers of precognition, feeble and sporadic though they were.

"How much armor have you taken?" asked Zen.

"All. Almost all," the old man conceded. "I have enough to make a trip into town and get supplies."

"Such scavenging will last you for many months, if I'm any judge," said Durril.

"Not so many. I sample the charms of the village." The old man turned sly, and his gaze darted about as if someone might overhear his small confession.

"I can guess what charms those are," said Zen. "And he'd have to pay a king's fortune unless he bathed first."

"How do you enter and leave the Valley of the Ultimate Demise?" asked Durril.

The ancient scavenger's mouth moved, but no sounds came forth. Durril increased the power of his spell of compulsion. The man had no choice but to reveal his path.

To his surprise, the man still did not speak, in spite of potent magics.

"His livelihood depends on the trail," said Durril. "He might die before he revealed it, even under my spell."

"What can we trade him?" asked Zen. "A deal is better than killing him, though he stinks like the dead already."

"Ghosts, even poltergeists, aren't as fragrant," Durril said with some aversion. To the old man he said, "I have a magical amulet to trade for the secret of entry to Rahman'dur's valley."

"What does it do?" the old man asked suspiciously. Durril bent close and whispered. The old man's eyes lit. "You would not fool me?"

Durril shook his head solemnly.

The scavenger looked at Zen, turned away and scratched a crude map in the dirt for Durril's eyes only.

"The amulet," he said, wiping out the map.

"Wait," said Zen. "Shouldn't we be sure of the path before giving him anything?"

"I trust him. He knows what will happen if he betrays a wizard while wearing this amulet." Durril worked through a box in the kit Zen carried. He took out a small silver bullet-shaped amulet on a chain and handed it to the old man. He took it, his hands shaking with eagerness. He hung it around his neck using the silver chain.

"It will protect you well against social plagues," Durril assured him.

"And the trail is safe, it is, yes, it is," the old man crowed. He scooped up his satchel and dragged it away.

"We might have our path into the valley," said Zen, "but you've turned loose a menace on the unsuspecting women of whatever village he trades in."

"We can return through that village and sell our magical wares. He might be protected from their women's diseases, but they'll need curing of whatever *he* carries."

Together, the master and the apprentice started along the path leading into the Valley of the Ultimate Demise.

Chapter 9

"Can you tell any difference between this trail and the one yonder?" Arpad Zen pointed across the ravine to the far hillside where a narrow trail had been cut through the rock. The trail they followed was strewn with large chunks of stone and walking proved difficult. The horses protested constantly as the sharp edges cut their hooves. Even Zen was not happy with the condition of path or feet.

"I see nothing guarding either," answered Durril. "The scavenger knew one safe path into the valley. That doesn't mean there aren't others unknown to him."

"That one looks easier," grumbled Zen.

"It might be. However, we stay on this one." Durril picked his way through the jagged rocks littering the path. He stopped when he came to a small stone cairn.

"A marker?"

"The old man said nothing about it." Durril drew his sword and poked into the stones with the tip. No angry protests from animal or insect resulted. He took away a few of the stacked stones and looked inside.

"Well?" asked Zen. "What is it?"

"A message box. There's a slip of paper inside." Durril pulled out the foolscap and held it up to the light. "I can't read it. The runes are in a style I've don't think I've ever seen."

"Is there an unlocking spell you can use to read it?"

"I don't think so, but now I look at it, it is starting to seem familiar." He looked around as he tucked the paper into his tunic for future study.

Below, along the ravine floor, moved wisps of ghostly guardians. He didn't think use of a weak spell would attract them, but he could not be sure. The risk of using any spell this close to the center of Rahman'dur's power outweighed the benefits.

"Is there a spell you can use to drive the ghosts away?"

"Short of complete exorcism, no," the master wizard answered. "Remember what the old man told us. Lord Northdell's entire army was vanquished within minutes. To overcome three hundred men required more specters than the thimbleful we see below us. The trap and the trigger are in the next valley over. These are simply watchmen."

Zen picked up a sharp stone that had cut through the leather sole of his boot. He held it for an instant, staring at the apparitions moving restlessly below. The urge to toss the stone almost overcame his good sense. He dropped it and turned to see Durril watching.

"Very good," his master complimented. "You learn restraint. Now you can build your muscles. Take the kit from the horse, and go down that slope. I'll join you in a few minutes."

Zen swallowed hard when he saw the sheer face of rock Durril had ordered him down. He slung the kit of magical appliances onto his back and gamely began the descent.

Durril watched for a few minutes to be sure his apprentice made good progress, then tethered the horses. From this point down into the Valley of the Ultimate Demise they would have to walk. He patted both animals and made sure they were within reach of enough grass to keep from starving for a day or more. If he and Zen hadn't returned by then, the horses' fate would be the least of his worries.

He made a slow circuit of the area, alert for any ghost that might be drifting past. Although he found ectoplasmic traces of recent ghostly movement, he detected nothing to show that danger awaited them. He did not trust the old reprobate, but so far his information had proven truthful.

Durril started down a different slope leading to the ledge just above the ravine. He slipped and slid a few feet, recovered and dug in his toes. A presence above made him jerk around and look back up. The spotted dog he had seen before stared down at him.

He began a spell to trap the animal then bit his tongue to stop it. More ghosts fluttered to and fro below. He did not want to alert them.

But what of the dog? It had followed him from Castle Northdell. He had seen it in the seaport. And it had been tracking him along the road leading to the Valley of the Ultimate Demise. Why? What forces commanded the small animal? That it was something more than a mongrel, Durril had no doubt.

But what? To that he had no answer.

"We'll meet one day, my little friend," he said softly.

The dog barked once and vanished behind the brink.

Durril got his balance back and continued down the slope. He came to the rocky ledge the scavenger had told him about and made his way along it until he arrived where Zen sat tailor-fashion, busily repacking the kit bag.

"What happened?" he asked softly.

"The load shifted on me. I'm rearranging our arsenal."

"Do not refer to my implements in that way," Durril said, more harshly than he'd intended. "A few can be turned into weapons. Most are healing spells or devices for improving the human condition. And never forget my master's skull is in the kit."

"Can he conjure a new pair of boots for me?" muttered Zen.

Durril heard him but paid him no heed. He waited impatiently until his apprentice had the bag repacked. Motioning Zen to follow, he went deeper into the valley using the ledge as a highway.

An hour's precarious hike brought them around the hillside and into the main valley. In the distance, haze turned the mountain peaks a dull, misty purple. Small dust devils disturbed the valley floor and made direct viewing impossible. Durril chanced a weak spell to be certain they did not blunder into an ambush.

"Nothing. The trigger for Rahman'dur's trap lies back in the valley mouth. We have passed it."

"Are there other traps deeper inside the canyon?" asked Zen.

"Probably, but none of the nature that brought about their deaths." Durril pointed through the dust at hundreds of bodies scattered along the valley floor.

Zen made a weak retching noise. "I'm all right," he said quickly. "I've never seen such carnage."

"I have," Durril said grimly. "The Spell Wars brought even worse. Wizards cast spells that ruined entire islands. The Plenn Archipelagos have never seen such death and destruction as was common in those sorry days."

Even though he *had* seen worse, the sight of Lord Northdell's slaughtered soldiers still sickened him. He fought down his rising gorge, not wanting to disillusion his apprentice.

"Has Rahman'dur turned them into ghosts?" asked Zen.

"I don't believe he has. There is a...presence when that is done. I don't sense the energy release. Rahman'dur commands vast numbers of apparitions. He shouldn't need more, unless he plans a major invasion of Loke-Bor."

"He hasn't in the years since the Spell Wars ended," said Zen. "Is there any reason to believe he will now?"

"Who can say what held him in this valley? Who can say what provoked him to send the ogre and other specters to Lord Northdell's castle at this time?" Durril scowled and rubbed his fingers over the hilt of his sword. He felt inadequate, in spite of his prowess with blade and incantation.

"Get a periapt from the kit. Cast an activating spell on it to alert you to ghostly presence—and nothing more. This will pass unnoticed by Rahman'dur because it is passive magic."

"How should it warn me?" asked Zen, taking a tiny gold medallion on a chain from the bag. Durril didn't answer. Zen thought hard, then cast the spell to warm the gold. Lying next to his skin, it would be silent but definite.

Durril nodded in satisfaction at his apprentice's choice. He turned back to the carnage on the battlefield. Taking a deep breath, he started down from the rocky ledge to the grassy sward, alert for Rahman'dur's ghost legion. He made his way to the first of the fallen soldiers. The body had been stripped of valuables.

"The scavenger has worked quickly and well," said Zen. "I hope the amulet you gave him causes boils."

"It prevents them," said Durril, paying little attention.

He went from body to body, seeking for any he knew. He had seen some of these men; most had been recruited outside the castle. They weren't trained soldiers. They were little more than green recruits who had followed their lord into a vicious trap.

"We should bury them," Zen said nervously. "After all, there are regulations requiring the disposal of the dead within ten days of their demise."

"Do it, if that's your pleasure," Durril said. "How long will it take to dig three hundred graves with your bare hands?"

Zen touched the periapt dangling around his neck. It had turned warm, giving warning of approaching phantoms.

"Let's hurry, master. The sun rots the bodies and causes a stench that turns my stomach."

Durril picked a path through the departed soldiers and found a small vale branching off from the main valley. He stared into the winding, misty depths and shivered, in spite of the stifling heat. Whatever Rahman'dur held in reserve in this valley commanded vast power and would be invincible against a human army. Even worse, once released, the spell could not be stopped by Durril, by him and Zen, by him and a hundred other wizards.

Rahman'dur played a deadly game to protect his privacy.

"Do we venture down there?" Zen stared into the depths of the side canyon with no enthusiasm.

"Straight ahead. There lies the destination of Lord Northdell and probably the Lady Kalindi."

Arpad Zen let out a gusty sigh of relief.

They continued hiking, keeping to one side to avoid occasional wraiths drifting by, caught and tossed on vagrant wind currents and hunting for interlopers. Durril held back the desire to exorcise each one he saw. He had no doubt that Rahman'dur activated spells everywhere to detect the use of any magic other than his own.

The valley was invincible against armed invasion. The other wizard need fear only magic.

"I cannot believe the old man risks his life coming into this place," muttered Zen. "The power of the magic all around is like a crushing weight on my shoulders. I fear to do anything more than hold my breath."

"And a good thing that is, too. It has been some time since you cleaned your teeth," said Durril. "Rahman'dur cannot watch constantly. He relies on his ghostly minions while he attends to other matters." The words sparked hot anger within him. Durril knew what those other pursuits must be. What did Rahman'dur do with Kalindi? The ogre had not kidnapped her for simple revenge. Rahman'dur could extract that from Lord Northdell by increasing the number of semisolid specters haunting his castle.

The wizard wanted Kalindi for his own purposes.

Durril clenched his hands until the cords stood out on his forearms as he thought of her fate. It had been five days since the ogre's attack.

He stopped suddenly and motioned Zen to one side. He turned his head slowly, straining to hear.

"What is it, master?"

"I'm not sure. Let's take cover for a few minutes. The rest will do us good."

"My feet are killing me," admitted Zen. "The stones on that ledge destroyed a perfectly fine pair of boots. See if I go to that cobbler in Wonne next time. He overcharged me grievously and—"

Durril waved him to silence.

The ground began to quiver and shake as if heavy siege equipment moved. Durril pushed aside the limbs of a low-growing shrub and slid into the center. He released the limb and green enfolded him. Peering through the leaves, he beheld a sight that turned him cold inside.

A ghost moved down the Valley of the Ultimate Demise, but such a ghost! The monster had feet longer than Durril was tall. Its thick legs looked like massive tree trunks. Its knees were huge and more heavily armored than any foot soldier in Lord Northdell's army. Its thighs were of a size Durril could never reach around with both arms. From the waist up he could see little because the tree tops hid the rest of the creature.

"What is it? I've never seen such a beast anywhere in the Plenn Archipelagos!"

Durril put his hand over his apprentice's mouth. Any monstrosity this size would have huge ears—and they might be acutely sensitive to small rustlings in the brush and frightened gasps from astounded peasants.

The lumbering ghost trod the length of the valley and vanished up the branching canyon that had worried Durril so much. This was only one of many magical creations Rahman'dur had conjured and hidden in that disturbing place.

The Valley of the Ultimate Demise was aptly named.

"It never lived!" cried Zen when the ghost was gone from earshot. "He never chained its spirit and locked its ectoplasm into this world!"

"No, it never lived," agreed Durril. "He has found a way of making ghosts without the need for killing living beings."

"I worried about him imprisoning Lord Northdell's army. Facing three hundred ghostly warriors would have been impossible," said Zen. "But he didn't need to do that, did he?"

"Rahman'dur has performed miracles in his seclusion." Durril couldn't take his eyes off the crossing canyon. What else awaited the wizard's command there? He shivered. He hoped he would never discover that.

"The ogre in the castle," mumbled Zen, thinking out loud. "Do you think it is a creation, too? I've never seen a living ogre, but I have heard of them all my life. Has Rahman'dur conjured the ogre's ghost from raw ectoplasm?"

"It might have been an experiment to practice before attempting larger ghosts," said Durril, his mind still on the towering apparition that had shaken the ground as it walked.

"Master, look at the tracks. It left tracks and—"

"Never mind that."

"Master."

Durril spun angrily, not wanting to stare at the evidence of passage. Then he saw what Zen had already found.

Smaller footprints in the middle of the monstrous ones were less than a day old. He dropped down and peered at them closely. Lord Northdell's crest appeared in the center of each heel imprint.

"Not far and not long ago," said Durril. "Good work, Arpad."

"We must go deeper into the valley?" Zen's voice cracked with strain.

"Not far. Look at the length of the stride. Lord Northdell was under deep compulsion. Rahman'dur moved him quickly. At this pace, he would have collapsed within a mile."

They hurried up the grassy valley, finding Lord Northdell's footprints in occasional muddy patches. Durril stopped abruptly and stared when he saw the young sandy-haired lord chained in the center of a grassy sward. The sunlight glinted off the slender links in the chain, and a golden lock secured him at the waist.

"Why does Rahman'dur leave him alone like this? He can break the chains," said Zen.

"Not if they carry a heavy binding spell."

"I sense nothing of the sort," said Zen. "He has cowed Lord Northdell into believing there is a spell."

"Perhaps not. Rahman'dur is cunning beyond reckoning. We've seen evidence of his handiwork and know he need not bluff when boasting of magical ability."

They walked slowly toward the chained lord. He looked up when he saw them, his face haggard and his blue eyes deeply sunken. His once-regal clothing hung from a body turned skeletal.

"You took your time finding me," Lord Northdell said in a dull voice. "Get me free. Now. Do it now!"

"A moment, lord," said Durril. "What manner of spell binds you in the middle of this field?"

"How should I know? All I want is to return to my castle." Lord Northdell sank to the ground and buried his face in his hands. "All I want is to be left alone. Rahman'dur can have the castle, for all I care. He can even take Kalindi, damn her!"

Zen touched his master's sleeve to keep him from striking the bound lord. Durril jerked free of the light grip and stood over Lord Northdell.

"You are a pathetic excuse for a ruler. Loke-Bor would be better off without you."

Lord Northdell looked up, a brief flash of haughty defiance on his grimy face. "You are in my employ. You failed to drive out the ghosts from my castle. You allowed Kalindi to be kidnapped by the ogre. You're the source of all my problems."

"Did we kill three hundred of your soldiers?" asked Durril, his temper barely in control. "Were we stupid enough to march into the teeth of a wizard's stronghold with only swords as protection?"

"Get me out of here. Free me, and I'll double your fee."

Durril snorted in disgust. He bent to examine the lock and fragile chains. He shook his head.

"I'll triple it! Get me out of here!"

"You could give us Loke-Bor, and I could not break this chain."

"It's a simple enough spell, isn't it?" asked Zen.

"No." Durril squared his shoulders and stepped back. "Break those links or force the lock and a spell is activated." He glanced back over his shoulder in the direction of the other canyon. "Whatever lies hidden back there will be unleashed if the lock is opened without using the key."

"Get the key, then, fool!" shrieked Lord Northdell. "Do it. I order you to do it!"

Durril stared up the valley, toward where Rahman'dur's fortress must lie. The only logical place to keep such a magical key was at the heart of the all-powerful wizard's dominion.

Chapter 10

"*Unlock the chains, damn your eyes! Come back and* do as I order you!" Lord Northdell strained against the short length of the chain binding him to the ground. The links rattled and clanked like a frustrated ghost haunting the halls of his castle, but the deceptively frail links did not break. The golden lock held firmly, too.

"Shouldn't we try to placate him to insure our continued employment?" asked Arpad Zen.

"Why bother? If we're not successful, he won't know the difference. He'll be dead, just as we will be."

Zen shuddered at the offhand way his master spoke. He looked around, as if he might see the vehicle of their destruction. Since the passing of the monstrous ghost returning to its valley post, they had seen no apparitions. It was as if Rahman'dur saved them for a real defense.

They walked in uneasy silence for almost an hour. Durril stopped suddenly and pointed ahead. His lips moved but no sound came out. Zen read, *There. Ahead. Rahman'dur.*

The apprentice clutched the kit bag containing the magical paraphernalia closer. He wasn't sure how to use most of the periapts and spells locked away inside, and his own grimoire was of little use. His master's might yield the proper spell, but he was unable to read the encoded spell book.

"He lives ahead. I sense the power that trails him like a miasma."

They advanced cautiously until they reached Rahman'dur's dwelling, located in a small clearing.

"That's where he lives?" Zen blurted.

"It seems incredible," agreed Durril. He refrained from using a spell to check the small thatched hut—an obscuring spell might have been cast to make a fabulous mansion appear other than it was.

But Durril didn't think this was the case. The sense he had depended on heavily since entering the Valley of the Ultimate Demise told him no spells cloaked the hut.

"A wizard capable of conjuring ectoplasmic creatures from nothingness can't live in a hovel like that!" Zen was outraged at the notion of a powerful sorcerer living in peasant's quarters.

Durril approached the hut. Beneath his feet, warmth grew until it threatened to burn through his boot soles. He noticed the magic did not affect Zen. Realization of the hut's true nature came to him. When he looked through the southernmost open window, his suspicion was confirmed.

No one lived in the hut. Rahman'dur lived *beneath* it—and Durril suspected the other wizard's true dwelling extended for miles in all directions. The hut merely covered the entry, protecting it from prying eyes. If Durril had attempted a scrying spell, he would have seen only this humble abode. An eagle flying above to spy on activities below would have seen nothing of Rahman'dur's true residence. Durril suspected, however, that any attempted use of magic would fail and show the curious snoop nothing.

"He has established ward spells on the doors and windows," Zen said, his hand hovering a few inches away. "Anyone entering will announce himself instantly."

"There are ways around such spells," said Durril. "They'll take time, but what else do we have at the moment?"

"But we can see there's nothing inside," protested Zen. "Why bother breaking into a peasant hut?"

"Arpad, my poor, witless apprentice, have you not seen the lengths a wizard goes to for privacy? Rahman'dur hides *under* this hut. If my estimates are correct, he lives in a fabulous underground cavern, with a city unlike any you've ever seen surrounding him."

Durril closed his eyes and remembered the soaring towers of ruby and jade he had seen in his nightmarish dream. That was Rahman'dur's true residence. And it lay beneath their feet; if only they could get into the hut and find the entrance.

"The door is as likely a spot to enter as any," said Durril. "The spell is homogeneous, and we'll not have to cut through thatch to get inside once the wards are thwarted."

He hunted in the kit bag until he found the implements he needed for the spell-casting. An hour passed as he spun the delicate and subtle incantation. He tossed a fine blue powder against the door. A round spot of utter blackness appeared amid a curtain of dancing blue motes. As the spell strengthened, the black circle expanded until it was slightly larger than man-sized.

"In," Durril ordered. "Take the instruments with you."

Zen scuttled through the black opening, dragging the kit bag behind him. Durril followed, careful not to touch the periphery of the spell hole. Inside, he relaxed the power of the spell, and the powdery motes danced in a solid curtain once more.

"Is this the entrance?" asked Zen. "It seems far too ordinary for a wizard."

"Stairs work for wizards and peasants, kings and fools," Durril said.

The simple trap door pulled up to reveal a black iron spiral staircase leading into the depths. He tested it for steadiness then descended rapidly, leaving Zen behind.

※

The apprentice looked about the hut nervously, thinking of what would happen should the monstrosity they had seen earlier happen by and peer inside. The darkness of the stairwell wasn't inviting, but it was preferable, he decided, to staying to confront the monstrous ghostly warrior. He scuttled after his master, bumping into him when he reached the bottom of the staircase.

"Isn't it everything I said?" asked Durril, his voice almost a whisper. He did not fear Rahman'dur hearing him or finding him with a spell. His soft-spoken words came from awe and admiration for Rahman'dur's tastes.

The spiderweb-like spires of lacy ruby and emerald and jade and diamond shone with an inner light. The buildings gleamed, and the streets of this huge hidden city were paved not with gold but a soft carpet that gave spring to the step as they walked along.

"The buildings are encrusted with precious gem-stones," murmured Zen. "Think of the wealth he accumulated to build such a fine city!"

"Some might be conjured as I do the gold coins, but not many," said Durril. "This is Rahman'dur's home and is not the product of illusion. He wouldn't tolerate counterfeit opulence."

"Where are we going?" Zen asked after several minutes of aimless wandering through the streets. "I saw a large building in what would be the center of the city. It had an emerald dome and golden pillars supporting its portico. Such a splendid building must be Rahman'dur's residence."

"I saw it, also," said Durril, "but the wizard is not the one we seek. If the key to Lord Northdell's chains can be stolen, we tread that path. Confrontation with Rahman'dur in his own city is folly—a deadly mistake."

"Wouldn't he keep the key with him?"

"Why? He has to maintain all this. His magical researches require vast amounts of time and effort. Watching after the simple key to a petty ruler's chains is a matter of indifference to a wizard such as Rahman'dur. He will have it with other keys, other unlocking devices for the city. Once we penetrate that room and steal all within it, we will have free run of his underground metropolis."

"You make it sound simple," complained Zen.

"It will be. In truth, it is so simple I am sending you by yourself to recover the key."

"*What?*"

"You said you desired more autonomy, and this is a mission of grave importance."

"To Lord Northdell, perhaps. I say he needs to improve his tan. Let him stay out in the sun awhile longer."

"That building. The one glowing pale red in reflected light from the pond. In there you will find the keys to unlock much in this city."

"What are you going to do while I'm stealing the keys?" asked Zen, fearing the answer. He cringed when he heard the words he had expected.

"The Lady Kalindi must be rescued, too. We allowed the ogre to steal her away. We must retrieve her."

"You're heartsick, master," Zen said. In a much lower voice, he added, "and a lovesick fool."

Such was Durril's preoccupation with the lovely woman, he did not hear.

"Will I be able to defeat Rahman'dur's guard spells?" asked Zen.

"Consider this a test of your abilities. The day had to come when you were on your own. We have no time to waste in this city. You get the key, and I'll fetch Kalindi."

"You know where she is?"

"Where else?" Durril's green eyes fixed on the domed palace.

Zen considered their different missions and decided he had the less risky one. He checked the kit bag and took what implements he could use. A quick tap on the hilt of his sword assured him it hung ready for use.

"Wish me luck, master."

"Yes, of course. Meet back here as swiftly as you can after you retrieve the key." Durril started off as if he had become mesmerized by the reflections off the green dome.

Zen watched his master depart. He heaved a deep sigh and steeled himself for the task ahead. He had studied hard, but Durril always chided him for lacking imagination. Stealing Rahman'dur's magical key would demand not only skillful application of spells, it would take inventiveness.

Arpad Zen's magical mastery was more than adequate for the task. He'd show Durril. He would!

The building with the key changed colors as he strode toward it, and the carpet beneath his feet lost some of its spring. Zen slowed to make a more careful examination of the building. The doors had been flung open in obvious greeting. This made him suspicious. Even in the middle of his stronghold, Rahman'dur would not leave doors unprotected.

A gentle, almost nonexistent observation spell showed faint blue wisps on either side of the doorway.

"Guardian ghosts," he murmured to himself. "This journeyman wizard is not so easily trapped!"

Zen worked his way around the structure. Each face of the building glowed with a different inner light. Blues and reds, peridot, burnt umber—the colors varied constantly. Zen frowned. Why bother with such conjuring unless it meant something?

Another spell, also subtle and of insignificant power showed the reason. Rahman'dur had left the code for entering the building in plain sight—any wall flanked by the same colors became an entrance, no matter that it appeared solid. Zen waited until the wall he faced turned purple and the walls on either side a bright green. He walked forward, never breaking stride, never doubting this was the proper way of entering.

He felt a tingling on his skin and then only the cool dampness of the interior of the building. He looked around for the key and was disappointed. He had expected to find it immediately.

"Lights," he said to himself. "There are too many dark corners." He clamped his hand over his mouth when he realized that the wispy specters at the doorway had responded to his words. They surged inward, then swayed and returned to their posts when he said nothing more and stood stock-still.

He explored cautiously, not even daring to light a torch he found in a wall mount. The room was larger than he had expected from studying the exterior walls. Holding his breath, hardly believing that he dared such folly, he conjured an observation spell of greater power than the one he had used outside.

The room lightened, and he saw the keys he needed—and the guardian watching over them.

"A cerberus dog!"

The exclamation drew the watchdog's attention. Two heads continued to stare at the keys hanging on a hook over a small tourmaline altar in a narrow alcove. The third head jerked around and focused cold, dark eyes on Zen.

He felt his soul being stripped away by this scrutiny. He dared not move—and couldn't had he wanted to. Fear paralyzed him.

"What have you done to me, master?" he moaned. This drew the attention of a second head. The bulky, powerful dog's body stirred and moved to face the intruder threatening to steal the keys.

One head barked; Zen wasn't sure which. He had alerted Rahman'dur's frightful canine. The heads bobbed around on slender necks, but he saw the corded muscles on the massive shoulders and the powerful, short legs. The cerberus dog wasn't bred for speed. It fought to the death and could bring down a dozen animals twice its size.

One head continued to bark, and the other two snapped powerful jaws in his direction. The light from his observation spell caused the two-inch-long fangs to glow a dull red. Zen found himself staring at them with hypnotized intensity.

"Avoid them. Fight it. How? A spell!" He fumbled among the implements he had with him. They were a pitiful lot, he realized. Durril commanded so many more spells—so many more powerful spells. How could he defeat a cerberus dog with the few pitiful incantations he had learned?

The observation spell began to fade, and the dog slowly melted into the darkness behind it. Zen hastily recast the spell. He dared not have an invisible foe attacking him, especially one this ferocious.

"A spell. I need a spell. Yes, the disappearance spell. That will do."

He placed a magic candle on the floor in front of him and lit it. Tiny particles of powders he had already combined fluttered down into the flame and sparked with all the colors of the rainbow. Zen concentrated on the chant, the words, the feelings of power that always welled from deep inside when he uttered this spell.

The cerberus dog inexorably advanced. All three heads snapped and barked now. Dashing past would be impossible. He had to reach the keys and get them from the hook, but the narrow corridor and the alcove with the altar prevented him from getting past the three-headed dog.

"Begone. Vanish. Get thee to another place!" he cried.

The cerberus dog yowled out a death cry and attacked. Zen dived and rolled, barely avoiding the left head's slashing fangs.

He found himself on the proper side; the keys dangled only a few yards away, but he didn't reach for them. The dog turned and advanced more carefully. Zen went cold inside. He had outfoxed himself. He had gotten past the guardian—and he had boxed himself in. The only way to escape was to slay the dog.

"My implements," he wailed. What magical instruments he had were on the other side of the cerberus dog.

Zen cast the spells he could without the focusing elements of the magical tools. The dog ignored them all. The last spell he cast before drawing his sword was the observation spell. He would be too occupied fighting to cast it again. He didn't want the magical beast vanishing on him while he wielded his sword in a futile attempt to cut off all three snarling, snapping heads.

"Master Durril has taught me well. Let's see if any of his fencing lessons are useful."

Zen lunged, his tip slicing the ear off the center head. The dog yelped, and the head jerked away. The other two used this opportunity to attack. Savage fangs from the left closed on the flat of his blade and sent fat blue sparks dancing into the darkness.

He recovered, twisting the sword and pulling it from the cerberus dog's mouth, hoping to cut important tendons. He did not draw blood. Only great agility on his part allowed him to avoid the right head's attack.

As he danced out of range, he grabbed the keys over the altar. He heaved a sigh of relief when he wasn't reduced to a smoking blob. He had worried that Rahman'dur protected the keys further with spells too clever for him to detect.

That the wizard depended on the cerberus dog to guard the keys did not hearten the apprentice. He was still pinned in a narrow corridor with the dog's blocky body filling the entryway. The three heads weaved and dodged as he cut at them. A new gash opened on one neck. The dog took no notice.

Zen remembered what Durril had learned about the ghosts' vulnerability to a steel-sharpening spell. As he fought, he cast the spell on his own blade.

He danced back and forth, keys in his right hand and the sword in his left. When the cerberus dog shifted position, Zen acted. He swung the sword with all his strength and felt the edge cut through the magical beast's neck.

The left head went bouncing out into the main room. The cerberus dog screeched in pain, and Zen again acted in a daring fashion. He ran forward, stabbed out to keep the dog off-balance and got one foot on the dog's back. He heaved with all his might and catapulted into the room, the dog behind him.

The cerberus dog roared in anger, got its stocky body turned around and again attacked. By this time Zen had scooped up his magical implements and saw the doorway opening in the wall.

He hacked away at the dog's necks as he backed out. A savage overhead cut landed on the center head and sent a spray of dark blood geysering up. Zen stumbled and fell through the building's wall, only a single drop of the blood touching his hand.

"Safe!" he gloated when he saw that the tri-headed cerberus dog did not follow—could not follow until the way opened again.

He got his feet under him and bounced the keys in his right hand, triumphant. The burning from the drop of the dog's blood on his left hand increased, though. He tried to wipe it off. It sizzled and popped and burned a hole in his tunic.

He started back toward the rendezvous spot, but the heat in his left hand spread and turned into an enervating flood coursing through him. He dropped to one knee, hardly able to stand. The triumph faded. Pain replaced it. He struggled to stand.

The cerberus dog's single drop of magical blood had felled him after he had endured so much.

The underground city spun in wild, crazy circles. Arpad Zen tried to cry out but even his voice left him. He crashed face forward into the street and lay there, unmoving.

Chapter 11

*Durril watched Arpad Zen head in the right direc*tion to get the key for unlocking the magical chains binding Lord Northdell. When his apprentice vanished from sight around the corner of a ruby-studded building, he started toward the palace with the green dome. Each step he took gave a new perspective on his destination. One angle caused the green dome to glow with translucence from within. A turn, and it appeared to be painted with shiny lacquer.

Closer examination revealed the glow to be coming from the material itself.

Durril admired the magics required to produce such an effect—and this was only part of what Rahman'dur had accomplished in the city. Feathery bridges arched from one tall spire to another. Durril wondered if it might be possible to walk from one side of the underground city to the other without setting foot on the ground.

He examined the carpeting under his feet more closely at that thought. The springy fabric robbed his tired muscles of their aches and pains. He felt invigorated simply strolling. The faster he walked, the more rejuvenated he became.

He stopped when he reached the point where he wanted to sing aloud and whistle and carry on like a small boy on a spring day. Too much ebullience robbed him of the watchfulness needed when dealing with a wizard of Rahman'dur's ability.

He ducked into a building located across a broad thoroughfare from the green-domed palace. Hunkering down, he touched the skull of his deceased master for luck then took out a few of the magical implements from the kit bag and placed them in a semicircle before him. A soft chant, a quick turn of a mirror, and he produced a scrying spell that penetrated the palace's walls and gave a murky, ever-shifting glimpse of all that happened within.

The specters guarding the interior of Rahman'dur's palace made Durril quake in fear. Never had he seen such ferocious apparitions. Tiny dancing-motes-of-light sprites darted everywhere. The slightest touch of a sprite meant painful, lingering death. The sprite expended all its ectoplasmic energy in the process and vanished, but the human victim suffered on.

Better to confront the stalking phantoms armed with all-too-substantial axes and morningstars. Durril had seen those before. He had exorcised several from Lord Northdell's castle, and they held little terror for him.

The true horror lay in the ghostly mixtures of beasts Rahman'dur had conjured. Durril suspected the other wizard of taking raw ectoplasm and forming it into his own creations, images of beasts that had never—could never have—lived. Odious creatures reminding him of griffins flapped on insubstantial wings down the corridors of the palace. Beasts of hybrid ancestry wiggled and stalked, swam and slimed along on their scaly bellies to protect the innermost suite of rooms.

In spite of his loathing for what he witnessed, it was on these rooms that Durril focused his full attention. Carefully expanding the scrying spell, he worked deeper into the palace. One noxious ghostly centaur trailed misty excrement as it galloped along the broad marble halls, a bow slung over one shoulder. The fierce expression on the creature's face told Durril it would die a thousand deaths before yielding one inch—and it was already a specter!

He hesitated in his conjurings as a strange and magical tide washed over the palace. Durril tried to find its source. He failed. The emanations came from deeper in the city, perhaps at a sub-level. He feared at first that Rahman'dur had detected him and sent undetectable magical alerts to the wraiths on patrol.

Whatever the reason for the surge in magical levels, however, it became apparent it had nothing to do with him. He waited until many of the guards had vanished on their rounds before scrying even harder. He doubted the ghosts were imbued with any magical powers by their creator, but he dared not risk one sensing his presence.

Durril's heart leaped to his throat and choked him when he saw lovely Kalindi sprawled on a large bed. She wore a pale pink gown of the filmiest material. He wondered if a mere touch would tear it—and he longed to find out.

The woman tossed and turned as if in pain. He saw nothing to inflict such agony on her. She sat upright in the bed and cried out, "I refuse to tell you. You cannot make me tell. And I'll never give them to you. Ever!" She clutched at the gold string of jewels and pearls suspended from her neck. The stones blazed with an intensity Durril found disquieting.

He had no warning of the attack. He toppled to his side as a powerful magical tide washed over the palace, directed against Kalindi. She gasped in pain and doubled up, shivering, on the bed. She clutched the bejeweled necklace in both hands and shrieked incoherently.

Durril forced himself to scry nearby locations. The focus of his spell was small—any larger viewing area would signal his presence. Two massive ectoplasmic constructs armed with shields and morningstars stood just inside the door to her room. Fighting them in any conventional manner would prove suicidal.

And magic? He knew the spells required to dissipate those guards would draw Rahman'dur's instant notice. Whatever the wizard wanted from Kalindi, she refused to give it to him. That meant his attention would be on her much of the time; he could not fail to notice another's magics.

Durril sighed. He had thought the worst of Rahman'dur in ordering his ogre to kidnap the woman, certain rape and servitude would be Kalindi's lot. Now it seemed that whatever had gone on before during Zoranto the Magnificent's rule had carried over into his son's—and the woman was at the heart of it.

What knowledge did Kalindi hide that a wizard of Rahman'dur's power might want? Durril had no idea.

He shook himself and rose, brushing off the dirt from his side where he had lain almost insensate. The scrying spell had drained his strength to a point where he staggered as he walked. Use of magic henceforth would have to be judicious, or he would never be able to rescue Kalindi.

He thought briefly of Zen and his apprentice's easy task of retrieving the key to Lord Northdell's chains. He, too, had been an apprentice once, and been given the menial jobs. He almost longed for those days now. Instead, he had to creep into this well-secured fortress and snatch away the lovely woman being tortured into revealing some dark and deadly secret.

Entry into the palace proved easy. He waited for the wraiths fluttering along on random air currents to drift by then slipped past. Their sensory impressions of the physical world were limited; Rahman'dur had set them to detect other ghosts, obviously fearing invasion by a spectral legion more than human incursion, believing himself secure because of his guardians in the valley outside.

Durril surveyed the massive entryway of the palace and gasped at its splendor. He paused to consider how fine life in this magnificent city must be. It could have been his, he knew. Instead of wandering around the Plenn Archipelagos, seeking out phantoms for exorcism, often assisting the peasant instead of always seeking out the wealthy lord, instead of living a meager existence, he, too, might have settled down and built a power base.

He shook his head. Such hoarding of power had led to the Spell Wars. He preferred the sea, and salt air in his face, the excitement of ever-changing isles, of meeting new people and friends and lovers.

His heart missed a beat again as he thought of Kalindi. A lover? He dared to hope she would return the affection he felt for her. After this rescue, how could she do less? Durril smiled wryly. She had admitted she had no love for Lord Northdell and that the marriage had been ordained long before either of their births.

Freedom of choice. That was the element in Durril's life that he would never exchange, not even for such majestic quarters as this gem-studded palace.

He heard wind whistling. He ducked behind a marble statue and peered around the base in time to see four small whirlwinds of ectoplasm whip across the floor. They bobbed and danced and intermingled to form a single larger tornado, then split and went down four different corridors radiating from the entry. Rahman'dur had patrols aplenty to preserve his security.

Durril began to enjoy the challenge of slipping past so many different types of ghosts. It mattered little whether Rahman'dur had conjured them from raw ectoplasm or had summoned their souls and bound them between worlds, the way most ghosts were trapped. They all obeyed the same laws. And Durril was a master. He knew the laws, and he knew the limitations on phantasms.

The centaur ghost presented the most difficult obstacle. It ran through the corridors at a speed unsurpassed by any of the others. It took less than a minute for the spectral beast to make a complete circuit to the fourth floor where Kalindi lay imprisoned.

Even worse was the ghostly excrement left behind by the diarrheic man-horse. Durril cast a mild observation spell and watched it glow a brilliant vermilion. To cross the moat of dung would mark him permanently—and he had no idea what spell burned in the clinging morass.

Ogre Castle

A spell to destroy the dribbling centaur-ghost was out of the question. He sensed the power locked within the ectoplasmic construct and knew Rahman'dur had lavished almost as much care on this creation as he had on the ogre sent to Lord Northdell's castle. Simple exorcism would never work, and might even turn on the exorcist. He couldn't shake the memory of the black lightning bolt the ogre had formed and thrown back at Arpad. Only luck and his master's quick thinking had saved the apprentice from a terrible death.

Durril waited for the centaur to trot past, positioned behind a door leading into a servant's room. He cast the most potent steel-sharpening spell in his grimoire until his blade glowed with a bright golden radiance that caused him to squint. Even such power would do little against the centaur-ghost, but he planned to use stealth rather than strength to bypass the guardian.

The centaur trotted past once more, tail raised and a steady stream of ghostly shit pouring out. The instant it rounded a bend in the corridor, Durril laid his blade on the floor and pivoted it back and forth. The crimson incandescence scattered before the magic of the spelled blade. Durril almost laughed at his good fortune in discovering this simple trick.

The clatter of hooves on the floor warned him of the centaur's return. He opened the door to Kalindi's sleeping chamber and dived inside.

He had the briefest of time to recover after he slammed the door. Then, the two massive spectral guards attacked.

Durril ducked under a morningstar blow and sliced through a vaporous shield and into the thigh hidden behind it. Tiny puffs of smoke rose from the cuts. In less than a second, the shield dissolved, leaving the morningstar wielder unprotected.

Durril lunged. The enchanted tip of his blade drove into an unseen heart. New puffs of foggy ectoplasm rose as he punctured the magical envelope holding together the ectoplasmic guardian.

"Behind you!" shrieked Kalindi.

From the corner of his eye, he saw the other guard using his shield as a battering ram. Durril danced forward, letting the shield push him along. He spun around the shield's axis and avoided the blow that would have left his head a bloody pulp. He clumsily poked at the ghost with his sword and failed to touch it.

Rolling along the floor, he avoided blow after crushing blow. He smashed hard against the bed, thinking it would offer some protection but saw his mistake instantly. The heavy morningstar rose and flashed downward, passing like steel through fog then turned into wooden hardness again when it touched the side of his arm. The impact sent him spinning across the highly polished floor and turned his left side numb.

"Rahman'dur warned me to stay on the bed. The ghosts cannot touch me on it. Jump up!" cried Kalindi. She clung to her necklace, fingers nervously moving from stone to stone.

Durril could barely stand. His left arm hung numb and useless at his side. He poked awkwardly at the ghostly guard's legs and held it at bay. This barely gave him the opportunity to roll back to the bed and fling himself across it.

He screamed as the morningstar rose above his head and came down blindingly fast.

Durril cringed as he awaited the blow that would turn his head to bloody mush. Only a whisper of wind blew against his face. He forced open his eyes and saw that Kalindi had spoken truly. The ghost guard was powerless to touch anyone on the bed.

He wasn't sure how that helped either him or Kalindi.

The towering ghost stalked back and forth in front of the door. Getting past it would be impossible now that the element of surprise had been lost.

"Lure him to the bed and use your blade on him," urged Kalindi. "I saw how it destroyed the other ghost."

"They may be powerful, but that doesn't mean they're also stupid," Durril said. The specter stayed just out of range of a sword thrust.

Even if he couldn't dispatch the ghost into the nether world where it belonged, Durril was content to sit and rub circulation back into his injured left arm. The blow had caught him high on the upper arm and left a bruise a full hand's-width in expanse.

"Let me help," said Kalindi.

He did not object as the pretty woman rubbed and stroked his arm. He winced in pain as she touched the spot where the ghost's spike-balled morningstar had landed. He said nothing for fear of causing her to stop.

"Rahman'dur has tried to question me ever since the ogre brought me here," she babbled. "I've refused to say a word. You'll rescue me, won't you?"

"That's why I came," admitted Durril. He wondered what their real chances of escape were. With Rahman'dur giving almost constant attention to the woman's questioning, it would be only a matter of minutes before the wizard discovered the interloper and summoned a full company of his spectral soldiers to dispatch him.

"I positively refused to give him my necklace, and I'll never tell him what he wants. I have no idea why he wants to know such things, but the ogre was terrible! It smelled and it gave me...things." Kalindi shivered in disgust and wiped her hands against the filmy gown, causing her lush curves to be outlined perfectly.

"What 'things?'" he asked.

"Bugs. Lice. It was a terrible monster!"

Durril blinked in surprise. He had never heard of a ghost carrying pests that preferred life on a mortal body. The ogre had been more substantial than a phantom, but it *had* been a ghost. This new information required closer examination.

All he had to do was escape Kalindi's sleeping chamber.

"How long before the guard summons others?" she asked.

"It might not be ordered to do so. They are difficult to train. The simpler the instructions, the more likely they will be carried out. Most naturally occurring ghosts follow a single route every night, repeating moans and chain clanks at the same places. The free-floating phantoms Rahman'dur conjures are much more difficult to guide. How he does it lies beyond my skill."

"I don't want you to direct them, I want you to kill them."

"Disperse or exorcise them," he corrected, as he might Arpad. "In the strictest sense, they are already dead."

He lifted his left arm and flexed the muscles. Pain stabbed him, but he knew he had to risk an attack.

Before Kalindi could respond, even to utter a cry of surprise, he shot off the bed and drove his sword tip directly into the patrolling ghost's throat. A geyser of mist erupted, sounding like a volcanic fumarole. It might have been a child's spring fair balloon the way the guardian ghost deflated and left only a thin fog hanging along the floor.

"You did it! We can escape!"

"Wait," he cautioned. "The *room* is clear. Outside is an even more dangerous specter."

Durril opened the door a crack and was sent reeling back when heavy front hooves kicked the door off its hinges. The centaur-ghost snorted in rage and reached for its bow and drew back for the kill.

At this range, Durril had no doubt the phantom arrow would sink into his heart and kill him instantly.

Chapter 12

Durril slashed wildly with the sword—and this saved him. The centaur loosed his shaft just as Durril's sword swung across its path. The enchanted blade caused the arrow to evaporate into mist when they touched. The centaur let out a bellow of outrage and nocked another arrow.

"Stop him. Don't let him kill me!" Kalindi cowered against the back wall of the room.

Durril fought for his life and hardly noticed her. He rolled and came to his feet, sword flashing. The cut severed the centaur ghost's bowstring. Durril had the curious sensation of moving through water; resistance met his blade and forced backward against his body.

He touched the centaur's body and rebounded as if he had struck a stone wall. The specter snarled again and groped for him. Durril cut off a hand, but the ghost did not bleed as the others had done. It was more substantial, and let out a bellow that might have been equine pain.

Durril fought to get the door upright and closed. The hinges were sprung, and the heavy wood panel hung awkwardly. Durril succeeded in forcing the centaur-ghost back.

"He's coming around the side!" warned Kalindi.

Durril smiled. In its physical shape as a man-horse, it defied his spell-enhanced blade. The instant it lost form and turned vaporous, he could defeat it.

Keeping his weight against the door panel, Durril began a simple spell. Wind whistled through the small chamber and caught at the ghostly tendrils. A distant neighing sounded. Durril changed spells. The filmy appendages seeking his flesh suddenly vanished.

Durril shoved the door aside and attacked a much smaller centaur ghost with his sword. Again he failed to cause the magical cuts that let out the ectoplasm, but the pain he inflicted caused an all-too-human wail to rise. The hoofed ghost hobbled off amid a flood of its own protective excrement.

"It's a good thing Rahman'dur didn't station a skunk outside your chamber door," said Durril, wiping sweat from his forehead. His hands shook in reaction to the battle, and his insides turned hollow with fear now that the centaur had gone.

"Let's get away from this awful place. I can't stand another instant here."

"Agreed," said Durril.

He poked his head outside and looked down the corridor. A solid wall of ghostly warriors were approaching. In the other direction it was even worse. Leading the well-armed ghosts trotted the faint, flickering centaur, now cut down to pony size but looking angry enough to take on a draft horse.

Durril ducked back into the sleeping chamber, not sure what to do. He knew this ruckus would draw Rahman'dur's attention, no matter what other tasks the wizard attended to.

"We're trapped," he told Kalindi. "There's no way to get past all the ghosts."

"No," came a rumbling voice, "there is no way. Who are you to intrude where you are not wanted?"

Durril's insides quivered with the force of Rahman'dur's voice. He did not bother answering. The other wizard would send a personal messenger with the death he had chosen for interlopers. Durril fought to keep calm. Panic only worked against him.

He conducted a quick inventory of the magical devices in the kit bag. He shook his head. Too few, too weak, not enough, not nearly enough. He sorted through the implements, picturing what spells they would bring into being and discarding them immediately. Outside in the hall, a roar grew as the ghostly warriors closed in.

Durril continued his methodical search. When he opened his grimoire he saw a slip of paper inside. It took a few seconds for him to realize what it was— the paper he had taken from the rock cairn they had discovered on entering the Valley of the Ultimate Demise.

"Die, fool!" cried Rahman'dur's disembodied voice.

Durril looked up in time to see a falcon with snakes for talons materialize. The ghost bird screeched, and its talons hissed and showed fangs dripping with misty death.

"Durril, save me. Do something!" Kalindi hung on his arm, preventing him from using his sword. Logic told him such a move would be useless in any case against such a powerful construct. Rahman'dur would not send a simple spell-generated ghost against another wizard who had penetrated this far into his kingdom.

The paper from the cairn held his attention. His eyes unfocused, and he stared at the paper...through it. Another world opened for him as he grasped the meaning of the spell written on the page.

Kalindi shrieked as the falcon banked and came in for the kill. Durril recited the proper line and turned sideways...and vanished from the sleeping chamber. Kalindi still clung to his arm, but they had been transported to another place and, Durril thought, another time. Or a place lacking the inexorable passage of time.

"Durril, there. It's coming after me!"

He heard the beating of the snake-falcon's wings before he saw it. The quick trip into this glass room had left behind most of Rahman'dur's deadly warriors, but not the serpent-bird.

Durril shoved the woman behind him and held her with his left hand. Using his right, he swung his spell-enhanced sword to keep the apparition at bay. The mighty beak clamped hard on his blade and wrenched with all the force of a physical, living, substantial being. As the falcon part wrestled the sword out of his grip, the snakes' fangs reached for his arm.

Durril thrust and lifted his arm out of the way of a savagely snapping snake's mouth. The edge of his sword cut across the falcon's mouth. As when he had attacked the centaur, foggy ectoplasm did not drift out. This was more a material being than a naturally occurring ghost.

"Durril, watch out!"

The woman's cry momentarily diverted two of the snakes. They shivered and shook at the end of the falcon's legs. Two other snakes continued their attack on the wizard.

He lunged again and felt fangs cut through his sleeve. The new thrust broke the blade in the falcon's beak and gave him a short, ragged-edged stabbing implement. He used it to cut the bird's throat.

The result was not all he had hoped, but the falcon did flutter back to regroup. It had diminished in size, as had the centaur after he attacked it. The snakes hissed and snapped and protested being removed so far from their victim.

Durril used the brief respite to look around. He had seen glass surrounding him, but what manner of place had they entered?

"It's all glass," he said, marveling at the room. The doorways were rimmed in beveled glass, and rainbows shone everywhere as light broke apart moving through the cut and angled planes. The furnishings in the room were similarly fashioned from glass.

"The creature!" warned Kalindi. "It's attacking again."

Durril glanced at it sideways and decided the ghostly construct had been severely injured and had developed caution toward him. He strolled through the room, fingers lightly brushing the furnishings.

"Do something. I order you to stop it!" Kalindi's voice became so shrill it almost broke with strain.

"It's thinking about attacking, but it'll wait a bit longer," he said. "And do not think to order me about. You're not yet lady of Northdell."

"Get me out of here. Immediately!" She stamped her foot and made the room ring like a fine crystal goblet. Kalindi jumped as the pure, clear note echoed through the room.

"Interesting," Durril said. "He must use this place as a testing ground. The ghosts are isolated by the glass. I'd never considered that before. This way. Hurry."

Kalindi bolted past him and crashed into the far wall when she slipped on the glass floor. Durril followed more cautiously, hand on the room's glass door.

The falcon let out a screech and attacked when Durril's intentions were obvious. The ghost crashed into the door and reeled back into the room. Durril smiled. It was effectively trapped in the glass room until the door was opened.

He looked for a locking device and found none. He decided the ghosts could not manipulate the doors.

Durril checked for ward spells and found none. Wandering the glassy corridors proved unnerving at first because he looked down three stories and more in places. The dungeons and lower levels were magnified and appeared to be just under his boot soles, but he quickly developed a feel for both walking and appreciating perspective.

"This is an awful place, terrible, I hate it," Kalindi muttered over and over.

"It saved us," he said. "Rahman'dur uses it to get away from ghosts. He has contrived a castle in which ghosts are effectively trapped and cannot roam. This must be his laboratory."

Even as he spoke, he worried that the wizard was somewhere nearby. All he had heard back in the sleeping chamber had been a voice without a physical body.

"How did we get here?" asked Kalindi.

"A good question, and one worthy of some consideration," he said. "The spell written on the paper opened the way. It isn't an easy spell. From its appearance, it might not be one that can be memorized and used at will."

"It must always be written down?"

"Perhaps," he said. "I could not read it yet was able to use it. Curious." He thought even harder. Why had Rahman'dur left it in the stone cairn?

A coldness clutched at his gut as he remembered where he had found the cairn. Rahman'dur feared his own conjurations, locked away in the side valley. So, the wizard had built in a safety route to get away from the ghostly juggernaut lying in wait. If the tidal waves of apparitions poured from the valley, Rahman'dur intended to be here in glass-enclosed safety.

In how many other locations around Loke-Bor had the wizard hidden the secret spell for reaching this haven? He feared greatly for his life if he left such a spell in plain sight. He risked exposing this wondrous glass castle to the curious glance of others.

Or did he? Durril shook his head. Who but Rahman'dur was likely to even enter the Valley of the Ultimate Demise? And there had been no other wizards on Loke-Bor since the end of the Spell Wars. His secret hideaway was safe from peasants and lords. Only someone who was a combination of wizard and adventurer would know of this place.

A wizard-warrior and adventurer such as Durril.

"He will figure out what's happened quickly enough," he said. "We've got to find my apprentice and be gone quickly from the valley."

"I approve," Kalindi said. "But why worry about your apprentice? He is capable enough to get free on his own. Let's go back to Castle Northdell without hesitation."

"It's not that easy, Kalindi. Lord Northdell is chained in the middle of the valley. Arpad has the key to unlock him. Without getting the two of them together, your future husband is doomed." He watched her reaction carefully.

"Leave him, darling Durril. We can rule Loke-Bor. You're a powerful wizard. Together, on the throne, we can rule twice as well as he ever could on his best day."

"A tempting offer, but one I am honor-bound to ignore at the moment. I still work for Lord Northdell."

"Work for me. Let's work together!"

She spun into his arms, staggering slightly as she lost her footing on the glass floor. He held her in the circle of his left arm and stared into her bright blue eyes. Those were orbs to imprison a man, he decided. He had seen worse ways of spending the remainder of one's life.

"We need Arpad to get free of the valley. Rahman'dur is alerted now and will have his entire legion of ghosts on patrol. If we set off even one ward spell, we are dead."

"We need him?" she repeated.

He nodded solemnly.

"Then let us find him and get free of this distressing place. I don't like it at all!"

"Take my hand." Her small hand in his, he drew forth the slip of paper with the shifting spell on it. He turned sideways, going backwards from the way he had before.

Durril stumbled. He tripped over Arpad Zen's body in the center of the street.

"Master?" croaked the fallen apprentice. "My sleeve. A drop of blood. Magical. Drains me."

"Don't talk." He cast an observation spell and saw the ugly red burn on Arpad's arm. The insidious curse had worked under the flesh and spread throughout his body. "Help me get him out of the city," he ordered Kalindi. "At least he has the key."

"Help? How?"

Durril heaved his apprentice up and got one of Zen's arms over his shoulders. He turned enough to give Kalindi the idea. She wrinkled her nose in distaste and said, "Is it safe? That revolting blood on his sleeve might get on me."

"It's spell blood and has found its host. You're safe from it. Now, help me get him moving."

Together, they half-carried and half-dragged Zen. Durril used his apprentice's sword to cut through several intruding ghost patrols. The steel-sharpening spell worked well and filled the streets with haze from the billowing ectoplasm.

"Why hasn't Rahman'dur come after us?" asked Kalindi.

"He might be in another place. His experiments might require all his time and effort at this moment. Or those might be far from the truth. I don't know. Let's make the most of his absence."

Durril continued to fight off the guardians and worry about Rahman'dur's real motives. What he had told Kalindi might be true. He kept at hand the slip of paper with the spell to shift into the glass castle, should he need it. Durril felt more confident fighting the other wizard in a place hindering ghosts. Even then it might not be an equal battle.

This was Rahman'dur's home. He had conjured the glass castle for his own purposes and must know everything about it. Durril had only taken a brief trip through and had skimmed, not studied.

"Here's the way to the surface," he said, heaving Zen

onto the first of the iron steps leading to the sunlight above.

"We were underground?" Kalindi asked. "I hadn't noticed." She turned and stared at the city's lacy spires and delicate, soaring architecture. "It *is* underground. All this is a magic city!"

"And one filled with ghosts intent on turning us into others of their kind," pointed out Durril.

He dragged Zen up the stairs. His apprentice tried to help, but the cerberus dog's blood had spread too far through his body. He was enervated and unable to walk.

"Daylight!" cried Kalindi. She stopped trying to aid Durril and ran to bask in the bright sun falling from above like rich, warmed cream.

"I can walk, master. Go on. I'll follow. Free Lord Northdell."

"What? We aren't leaving here immediately?" Kalindi stood, stunned. "How dare you risk my life in this manner? I demand that you take me home."

"Help him," Durril said.

Zen clung to the woman. She tried to shove him away but he had enough strength left to hang on for his life. Kalindi helped him follow the wizard but did so with ill-grace.

Durril ran ahead, keys in hand. All around he felt phantasms rising in response to the keys' theft. He studied the ring and found the smallest one. It had to be the one that worked on Lord Northdell's lock.

"Here!" came the faint cry. "Over here, Durril. I need you. Help me, please, help meee!"

Lord Northdell's voice weakened and trailed off. Durril hastened to the young ruler's side and dropped to his knees.

"I'll have you free in an instant," he promised. He thrust the key into the lock and tried to turn it.

It failed to open the lord's bonds.

Chapter 13

"*The lock won't open!*" *exclaimed Durril. He tried* forcing the key to turn. It didn't budge. He cursed, and sweat began to pour from his forehead as the strain mounted.

"Help me," begged Lord Northdell. "I can hardly move. The sun's too strong. The ghosts torment me. I can't take it. Open the lock. Free me!"

"I'm trying." Durril tried each key on the ring, and most wouldn't even fit into the keyhole. In frustration, he tried the smallest key again—and again he failed to win the lord's release.

"Why are we doing this?" came Kalindi's querulous voice. She saw her betrothed in chains, and her tone changed. "My love! What have they done to you?"

"It's Rahman'dur. The wizard took me from my army."

"He *slaughtered* your army," Durril said viciously. "You led them into the valley, and they were all massacred."

"His ghost warriors were too strong. Help me, lovely Kalindi." He held out his arms to her. She tumbled into them while Durril continued to struggle with the recalcitrant lock.

"It won't open," he called out to Arpad Zen. His apprentice looked worse than ever, although some strength had returned. "It won't even turn. Are you sure you got the right key?"

"I can't say. These were the only keys I detected." He outlined his magical detection work. Durril nodded in agreement. He could have done no better.

"What manner of stone comprised the altar?" Durril asked.

"Tourmaline."

"There must be a clue to the spell to use to turn the key. Did you see any runes, any markings, anything to give a hint?"

"A single letter." Zen drew it in the dirt.

"Utter the letter as you turn the key," Durril commanded.

"I am too weak."

"Do it. He who takes the key must be the one who uses it. It is Lord Northdell's only chance."

Durril looked around nervously. Curious apparitions floated past to study them. How long would it take before one reported back to Rahman'dur? The wizard might have misplaced them for the time being, but with so many free-floating spies in the valley, he would soon find them again.

Already, Durril saw armed ghost warriors milling around the edge of the field where the lord was chained.

"No good, master," moaned Zen. "I tried and failed."

Durril laid his hands on Zen's shoulders. "Once more. Try once more," he urged.

The weakness in the apprentice's body flowed into him; energy flowed back. On the first try, Zen opened the lock, and the chains fell away.

"Free!" exulted the ruler of Loke-Bor. "Now we can get out of here. I want nothing more to do with my father's mortal enemy. Let Rahman'dur stay in isolation, if he leaves me alone."

"That's not the way this misadventure started," reminded Durril. "Rahman'dur came after you. Remember the ogre? Remember the specters filling your castle? Remember how you cowered in your ghost-blood-filled study?"

"Nonsense. I merely studied their patterns to select the best method of disposing of them," Lord Northdell said. He held Kalindi close. "We will return to the castle and be married now that you have put this upstart wizard in his place."

Durril's eyes widened in amazement. The young lord had no notion of who wielded the power on Loke-Bor. The best he hoped for was escape with his life. Rahman'dur commanded every creature, both mortal and supernatural, in the Valley of the Ultimate Demise.

"Oh, yes, my lord," sighed Kalindi. "A wedding. We can have the wedding right away, and I can sit beside you on the throne."

She flashed a hot look in Durril's direction, as if to say that she only humored Lord Northdell. Durril had no idea what went on in her pretty, conniving head. His only goal at the moment was to escape. Quickly.

"They come," groaned Zen. "All around us, they come."

"Help him," Durril snapped, pointing to Zen.

Lord and lady looked offended at the notion of even touching anyone so afflicted. Durril's cold gaze forced them into action.

"What are we to do?"

"Arpad will guide you," Durril said, wanting the pair to keep Zen alive to benefit from his knowledge. They would abandon him if they found the way out by themselves.

He whispered in Zen's ear, "Go directly to the old scavenger's path and take it out of the valley. You know the way."

"Yes, master. What of you?"

Durril watched the legions of deadly specters moving toward them. "I'll hold back Rahman'dur's helpers. Hurry. There is little time."

He saw the paleness and fevered glow in Zen's eyes and knew the cerberus dog's blood worked its insidious magic. Within hours, Zen would die unless a countering spell or an antidote was found.

Durril regarded the advancing ghost army with some trepidation. Zen would die in hours *if* the ghostly warriors did not slay them all in the next few minutes.

He held Zen's sword in his hand. It balanced wrong for him, having been fashioned for the left-handed apprentice. He worked a new steel-sharpening spell and saw the golden glow along the cutting edge intensify. This gave some small protection he had previously lacked.

But how could he fight hundreds of Rahman'dur's spirits? There seemed to be no way to hold them back while Zen and the royal couple escaped.

He backed up and began muttering the most powerful exorcism spell he knew. Such potent magic drew attention. Ghosts drifting past on vagrant wind currents turned to face this threat. One or two of the nearest popped! out of existence. The mass of the army marching down on him never broke stride.

Durril crossed the width of the valley to divert the ghosts from the others. He failed. Part of the legion marched after them and the rest came for him.

He smiled without humor. His work had become harder, but the ploy had been worth the effort. He might have succeeded in giving Lord Northdell time to get up the old man's secret trail with Zen.

"Hai!" he cried, rushing forward. He saw no reason to die without trying to dissipate as many of the ghosts as possible.

His enhanced blade flashed left and right. Each cut caused the misty bleeding that meant the eventual dissolution of the phantom. He fought with frantic need. Ethereal swords cut at his head and arms and legs. Some wounds opened. Durril ignored them and fought with renewed strength. As he worked his sword in broad circles and short, quick thrusts, he conjured every exorcism spell at his command.

It took him several seconds to realize that he was thrusting at thin air, that his spells no longer worked—because every phantasm facing him had been vanquished. Panting, he bent over, hands on his knees. Zen's left-handed sword had raised blisters on his hand; these were the least of his worries. The cuts from the phantom blades bled profusely, as if made by steel. Covered with blood, he sank to the ground and worked what healing spells he could without tiring himself even more. He had to conserve strength for the real fight.

The worst of the bleeding stanched, he rose onto shaky legs and took several deep breaths. In the distance, from the direction of the tiny hut masking the entrance to Rahman'dur's fabulous underground city, came a steady stream of new phantoms. He wondered if they were natural ghosts composed of thin ectoplasm or if they were the hardier, more-difficult-to-dispatch constructs conjured in Rahman'dur's laboratories.

Finding out would put more than a strain on his abilities. They would wash over him like Mother Ocean's surf washed over a sandy beach. He would be no more than a tiny grain of sand struggling against the sea.

Durril limped at first, then ran with stronger strides to catch up with Zen and the others. The rear echelons of the ghost army pursuing the trio parted for him as he slashed his way through. Tiny moving dots on the hillside marked the progress Zen, Kalindi and Lord Northdell. The ghosts did not follow them, milling about at the base of the hill.

Durril suspected why this stretch of land in the Valley of the Ultimate Demise prevented the specters from patrolling, and why Rahman'dur had not conjured his ward spells. Some portions of land refused to allow any spell to be cast above them; he had never learned why. His master had not known, and he had never been interested enough to do the research required to find out.

He was sorry now for this lack of imagination on his part. It might save his life—and those of the other three.

The specters were slow in realizing where the danger came from. When they sensed him and turned, they responded with more speed and determination than Durril liked. He was soon fighting just to stay alive.

The spells he wove around them kept the fiercest of the ghosts at bay, but such conjuring took its toll. He weakened even as he gained some room to maneuver and fight.

He considered turning and running until he glanced back and saw new waves of reinforcements coming. His master's favorite saying stuck in his mind: Better to die with an arrow in your forehead than in your back.

"I'll die fighting!" he cried.

A frenzy of cuts and slashes opened a small channel through the ocean of ghosts. He felt his legs giving out under him as he rushed forward, sword swinging. He was being cut to bloody ribbons by the ghostly swords.

When a heavy mace glanced off the side of his head, he staggered. The world exploded into spinning points of dazzling light—and this saved him.

Durril blundered forward, swinging the sword wildly. He stumbled over a large rock and fell. For several seconds, he lay flat on his back, staring up at the sky. When he recovered his senses he saw he had won through to the protected ground at the foot of the hill. The ghosts stabbed at him futilely, and others with maces swung, missing him by inches.

Whatever strange spell permeated the mountain, it had saved him, just as it had already saved Zen and the others,

Durril scooted farther up the hillside and regained his feet. The ghosts shrieked and whined like wind through cracks in a castle wall. He ignored them as he ascended the hill, occasionally slipping but taking pains to make sure he didn't tumble back into the ghosts' deadly grasp.

It took him longer to reach the top of the hill and the rocky ledge than it had to enter the Valley of the

Ultimate Demise. Durril didn't mind. He was safe...for the moment.

He hastened along the lower ledge, climbed to the upper and followed it. He stopped in his tracks when he saw Arpad Zen sitting with his back against a large rock.

"Arpad! What happened? Where are Kalindi and Lord Northdell?"

His apprentice opened his eyes but could not focus properly. His lips moved; choked, tiny animal noises came out.

"The pair of royal la-de-dahs left him once they saw how to get back to the main road." The old man sat atop a nearby rock, watching like a vulture. "Didn't care spit for him, no, sir, not at all."

"They *left* him?" Durril was shocked.

"That they did. The pair of 'em went off arm-in-arm, cooing and billing like a pair of gaudy lovebirds."

Durril's wrath grew instant by instant. Zen had risked his life to save them, and they had abandoned him.

"I can look after him for you, I can, I can," said the old scavenger, "but he's not got long for this world. Seen another like him come staggering out once. The rot's inside and spreading fast."

"The rot is in more than my apprentice," Durril said, looking back into Rahman'dur's valley.

"You're not thinking of doing anything stupid, are you now, old son?"

"I know what must be done. Whether I can do it is something only trying will tell."

"I'll look after your young friend, good and proper, I will. You get back there and roust Rahman'dur. He's been needing it since the end of the Spell Wars. He carries on like some type of royalty, he does."

Durril turned cold inside as he thought of returning. The army of ghostly warriors, the magical traps—the torrent of the unknown waiting to be released in the side valley—all filled him with dread.

Yet, not stopping Rahman'dur now would prove the more dangerous course to follow. Durril gathered what magical implements he had, arranged them, touched Zen to give him a moment of comfort and assurance, then started back into the Valley of the Ultimate Demise.

Chapter 14

Durril stopped on the hillside and surveyed the horde of ghosts. They slashed the air with vaporous swords and swung substantial maces with enough power to crush his skull. They were a strange collection of film and substance. He studied them, deciding which were natural ghosts and which Rahman'dur had constructed from gobs of raw ectoplasm.

The remnants of the Spell Wars had a tired, beaten look about them. The aggressive, vicious ones that were more difficult to see through carried the other wizard's cachet.

A howling like wind in tall trees rose. The ghosts surged forward, Rahman'dur's unseen order to attack forcing them up the hill. Durril stood his ground. As they crossed an invisible line at the base of the hill, they vanished. Tiny moans of pleasure or pain intensified. Durril saw that the Spell Wars remnants rejoiced in their extinction. Rahman'dur's constructs experienced agony as they dissipated.

He sat and pondered his course of action. He remained safe if he did not move, yet the pressure of time forced him into action. Arpad would die unless he found a counter-spell to the cerberus dog's deadly blood.

On a grander scale, he had to stop Rahman'dur from releasing whatever he had penned up in the side valley. The force of evil radiating from those peaceable-looking canyons made Durril twitch. The Spell Wars were over but not forgotten. He feared Rahman'dur intended to bring back the horror of those long and terrifying years.

Unconsciously, he began arranging the few implements he had with him. He placed the spell candles around his master's skull in a strange configuration, one he had never tried before. He sprinkled ground bison horn with a pinch of tricorn blood in it between the candles. The tiny wax tapers burst into flame without him touching them. A slow smile crossed his lips. He had found still another new configuration of powers.

He muttered a spell of binding, then louder called, "You are mine to command! Turn on those who do not obey me!"

He hastily gathered his implements and stood watching what occurred across the valley. The remnants, those ghosts left from the Spell Wars, turned against the constructs Rahman'dur had conjured. Ghost fighting ghost produced strange casualties. Some of the natural specters vanished in tiny puffs of mist. The heavier, more substantial constructs collapsed into murky, churning piles of fog that lingered at ankle height.

There could be no turning back now. Durril hastened into the Valley of the Ultimate Demise while his spell bound the remnants. They would not follow him—Rahman'dur's control was too strong—but he could turn them against their unnatural companions. He played on animosity among the ghostly dwellers in this valley that must have built over the years.

Unchallenged, he reached the pitiful hut that hid the entrance to Rahman'dur's underground city.

Durril took a deep breath. He had recovered most of his strength, both physical and emotional. It took so much out of him when he conjured. And getting Zen to safety had pushed his strength to the limit.

The thought of Arpad suffering from the single drop of cerberus dog blood coursing through his veins turned him cold inside. Power welled up and pushed aside the small parts of Durril that refused to respond to anything less. Rahman'dur had put the animal on patrol; he knew the antidote to the insidious poison.

And he would yield it, by force if necessary.

"You are a fool," came Rahman'dur's disembodied voice. "A brave one, granted, but still a fool. You think the pathetic army of apparitions I set wandering my valley are the only defense?"

Durril did not bandy words. He conjured quickly and examined the ward spells in place around the hut. He brushed aside one and entered. It took him only minutes to race down the spiral staircase and go into the vast, glowing, beautiful underground city.

He turned slowly, like a compass needle seeking a pole. Power emanated from the green-domed palace in the center of the city. He had not expected Rahman'dur to make his stand anywhere else, yet he had to check. The brief examination revealed other danger points. Bright red glows surrounded the two worst areas. One building so marked had contained the keys Arpad had

stolen to free Lord Northdell. The other stood antipo-
dal. Durril thought on this and decided much of
Rahman'dur's power came from the opposition of
forces. The magical energies from the two points focused on the green dome and became his to command.
Destroy one pole and the other would be useless for
feeding the wizard's might.

Durril began conjuring, locating the ghosts left
over from the Spell Wars. It had worked once for him
and would work again. Rahman'dur's contempt for this
trick made it likely the other wizard would hide behind
a wall of his own ghostly constructs.

But Durril did not match ghost against ghost. He
sent sprites and goblins and wraiths and any other free-
floating specter in the city against one pole of
Rahman'dur's energy generator. The building where
Arpad had stolen the keys and run afoul of the cerberus
dog struck him as an appropriate spot to mark for destruction.

"You dare come to me? You are not brave. You
transcend foolishness. You lack all common sense!"

Durril waited to see what portion of the phantoms
in the underground city obeyed his magical order. He
smiled more broadly when he saw that more than half
did. The constructs remained close to the green dome.
Rahman'dur trusted them more than the natural
ghosts; they were loyal because he had given them their
pseudo-life in his magical laboratories.

"What power do you hide in the valley?" Durril
asked.

"Since the Spell Wars ended, I have worked on conjuring a ghostly force no one can defeat. No one! I will
rush forth when I am ready and conquer Loke-Bor.
From here, I will establish my base and spread across

the Plenn Archipelagos until all islands tremble at the mere mention of my name!"

"Grandiose schemes for one unlikely to vanquish a simple itinerant wizard," Durril said.

"Die, worm!"

Durril had readied his strongest defensive spell. He had thought Rahman'dur would attack with his legion of phantasms. Thunder warned him of a different spell, a different attack.

A slight shift in the chant created a wall of the purest blue mist in front of him. The thick black spear that drove straight for his heart embedded in that wall— and quivered and twitched and dug deeper. He tried to dissipate it. He failed.

Durril was a master and did not panic when his spells failed to destroy Rahman'dur's death bolt. He continued to work as the magical black spear inched toward him. Fleeing would do no good. The spell had been conjured for him and him alone. Run as he might, this blackness would seek him.

Better to die with an arrow in the forehead than in the back, he reminded himself.

The barbed head of the inky missile penetrated his shield. Durril reached out and touched the tip with his finger. A drop of blood flowed as he pricked his index finger.

The blood exploded the spear with such violence he staggered away. Both shield and Rahman'dur's weapon vanished.

"Legions, march on him. Destroy him!"

Rahman'dur had issued the command Durril would find the hardest to counter. Hundreds, perhaps thousands of ghost constructs would come for him. He could not exorcise them; they were closer to living beings than normal spirits. Touching the spell-enhanced sword he had taken from Zen failed to give him any confidence.

Durril forced his mind to go blank. Thinking was not the course for him. Reaction was. He had trained all his life to be a wizard. Unconscious response would save him. The right spell would rise unbidden to his lips, as it had before when he pitted one faction of ghost against the other.

He responded to the first specter with a quick twist of his wrist. The tip scored the construct on the cheek as he uttered a dissipation spell. The manufactured specter melted like butter in the noonday sun. Durril stepped over the sticky mass of ectoplasm on the ground and advanced.

Such confidence caused the ghosts to pause for a brief instant. Rahman'dur's voice bellowed at them to attack.

Every second's delay was important to Durril and had won the day for him. The remnants he commanded had entered one pole of Rahman'dur's magical power generator and had...

Words failed him. He envisioned the ghosts flinging themselves forward and vanishing in puffs of ectoplasm. This stream of entities against the magical generator destroyed it. Not one ghost or a dozen dissipated itself at his command. Thousands did.

Durril staggered under the realization of the power of Rahman'dur's ghost legions. The rogue wizard had not needed a new and more powerful weapon to conquer Loke-Bor—or the world. These specters would have proven sufficient to reduce all but the most determined human armies to masses of fleeing individuals.

The constructs surrounding him began to dim and turn transparent. They waved their swords and swung morningstars, but the weapons dissolved into misty nothingness. Durril walked through the center of Rahman'dur's army and felt only faint puffs of wind against his face and hands.

"What have you done? You cannot upset the delicate balance of my power like this! You don't know what you're doing!"

Durril did not respond verbally. He fashioned a spell of his own and sent it against Rahman'dur's green-domed palace. The magical energy flow had become unbalanced. He nudged the weakened side with a movement spell. Cracks appeared in the side of the building.

Durril blinked in surprise. This was more than he had anticipated. The green dome did not crack so much as it dissolved. Sugar in water vanished quickly. If the green dome had been constructed of strangely colored sugar and were the air around it water, it could not have disappeared faster.

Hysterical shrieks echoed across the city and died. Rahman'dur no longer magnified his voice magically. His power waned as the buildings were destroyed.

Durril did what he could to hasten the magical demolition.

"You will not win, wizard!" shrieked Rahman'dur. "Your apprentice dies. Only I have the antidote. You've destroyed my city. You'll suffer through the years knowing you killed him! You killed my city and you killed Arpad Zen!"

"You have the antidote?" Durril asked in a soft voice. He put every bit of his persuasive power into it. Some of it might have been magical. Most was the tone he used during his raree show. Selling small magical cures and exorcisms had been his job for many years, and he was good at it.

The hints of persuasion carried through and worked subtly on his enemy.

"It's here, fool. I carry it in a locket around my neck. And I am going to destroy it. You've doomed him. Doomed him!"

With the underground city melting into slag all around him, Durril advanced steadily. He saw a lonely figure on the steps of the palace. All around him lay the green dome, reduced to dust. It had evaporated into the air and then fallen in minute particles the size of grains of sand.

Yet, in some fashion he did not understand, Rahman'dur still absorbed power from the dome.

Durril conjured a small wind demon that whipped up the sand and carried it into the dissolving city. Rahman'dur shrieked in rage when he felt even more of his power vanish.

"You won't get this. You won't!" He held a locket high above his head.

Durril paused, then said, "A trade, master."

"What?" This confused Rahman'dur. "What are you saying?"

"A trade. You can let Arpad die in exchange for the destruction of the force assembled up the side valley."

"What are you saying?" Rahman'dur laughed harshly. "I will do as I please. He will die *and* my magical tide will wash clean the isle of Loke-Bor!"

The wind demon had swept away the last of the green dome that gave Rahman'dur his power. After it had gone, he was no more powerful than Durril—and far less intent. Rahman'dur squandered his focus, lost his concentration and allowed Durril to distract him.

Durril issued a simple exorcism spell and brought Rahman'dur to his knees.

"My city. My lovely city. You've done this. I–I'll release the tidal wave of ghosts."

"No," Durril said gently. "All you'll do is die."

He took the locket from Rahman'dur's trembling hand. A single thrust with the sword severed important arteries in Rahman'dur's throat.

Durril stepped back and avoided the sanguinary flood. The locket resting in his palm, he spun and hurried from the city. Only rivers of slag flowed to remind him of the proud and soaring towers. Blackened lumps remained where had once stood works of art that had impressed him.

He did not care. Rahman'dur had built beauty to create evil. His death had been a quick and merciful one, more than he deserved.

Durril reached the spiral staircase just as the cavern ceiling began to crack and huge hunks of jagged rock fell to the ground.

Chapter 15

Durril thought he was going to faint, then realized *he* was not shaking—the tremors came from below. Rahman'dur's underground city had dissolved and turned into molten slag. All around, he watched huge chunks of the gently rolling plain fall like waves in a storm-tossed sea. The rocky vault over the city collapsed in frightening slow motion.

He hurried, knowing that, otherwise, he would end up in the city again in a way not pleasing to him. At the edge of the grassy sward, he turned and saw gigantic pieces of pasture land vanish from sight as they tumbled into the city. He bowed his head for a brief instant. Rahman'dur had been a powerful wizard and had conjured well.

Perhaps too well. The success of his magic had twisted his ambition and brought back the corruption so many had experienced during the Spell Wars.

Durril broke into a dead run when the valley sides began to slip and crumble. The dissolution of the subterranean city had pulled down more than the vault over it. The stony walls creaked and moaned and began to show cracks large enough to march an army through.

He paused when he came to the side valley where Rahman'dur had prepared his ghostly horde. What form did it take—and how could he neutralize the spells giving it structure? Power of awesome magnitude radiated from the direction of the vale; Durril hesitated to investigate and find out what Rahman'dur had created.

He believed his own life would be forfeit if he ventured too far. *The Valley of the Ultimate Demise,* Rahman'dur and the inhabitants of Loke-Bor had called this place. Durril juggled the small locket containing a few grains of powder in his hand. Rahman'dur had claimed this potion would save Zen from the cerberus dog's blood. To embark on a trip that might end in his death doomed not only himself but his apprentice.

Durril tucked the locket away inside his tunic and started down the ghost-crowded valley. On left and right, ghosts struggled—the thinner ones remnants of the Spell Wars and the denser ones Rahman'dur's creations. He smiled. His single impulsive spell had proven to be the key to unraveling the entire evil domain.

The smile faded as he rounded a curve and confronted the invincible tide of apparitions Rahman'dur had conjured. The constructs all matched the towering giant in size and the ogre walking the halls of Castle Northdell in ferocity. He had blundered into their training ground.

Durril tried to find a description for this congregation of phantoms and failed. They wrestled with one another, more physical substance than ghostly. Flails and rods and maces swung and mashed heads. The victims tumbled and dropped, only to reform their damaged skulls and rejoin the fray. An army of these behemoths could crush any human legion.

He slipped off the main path and crouched against a steep, rocky canyon wall. Exorcism would never work against so many constructs. Rahman'dur had worked diligently for many years to produce more than a hundred of these not-quite-ghost creatures.

For the first time, Durril doubted his own sanity. He should have hurried to Arpad's side and saved his apprentice. Even though the pair of them could never defeat such an army as he now observed, they might have done more together than he could do alone.

He frowned as one giant swung a sharp steel sword and severed the arm of another construct. Blood spewed forth, and the injured ghost wailed as if he were human and had lost a real arm. The blood did not have the appearance of ectoplasmic fluid, which always rose in a lazy smoke-like spiral. This looked physical and real—it looked like any human's blood.

Durril slipped along the rocky cliff face and darted out to touch the blood, pooling in a shallow depression, becoming deeply engrossed as he examined it. He cast several spells, then looked up in astonishment.

"They're becoming physical beings. Rahman'dur's death has released them from their ghostly existence."

He almost laughed aloud. Soldiers this size would fall easy prey to a squad of archers. No matter how fleet of foot they were, their sheer bulk would prevent them from avoiding flight after flight of arrows. A few well-chosen poisons or spell-tipped missiles would fell even the most powerful of these hulks.

To prove his point, Durril fashioned a sling from strips of decorative rawhide lace taken from his boot tops. A sharp rock and a trenchant spell completed the equation. He slung the rock as hard and accurately as he could. The enchanted rock grazed the temple of one lofty giant; the construct touched the spot, and his hand came away bloody.

He began to yowl and spin. A sudden stiffness in his joints caused him to topple like a tree with its trunk cut. Durril watched in satisfaction as the giant died.

Ghosts could not die—they were already spirits of the dead. This construct had become alive when its creator died. Whatever bonds held it to the spectral world had vanished with Rahman'dur.

Durril started conjuring more deadly spells for use against the once-invincible army. Spells would have been pointless against ghosts of such stature, and no human warrior could have slain one. However, he found the chore almost easy.

He finished his conjuration and surveyed the canyon walls. Tiny cascades of dust marked where his spell began. It ran into the rock face and brought down a tiny stream of pebbles. By the time the now-living giants understood that the walls were about to collapse on them it was too late.

Durril ran from the canyon, the thunder of the landslide filling his ears. He skidded to a halt in the mouth of the valley. With regard to Rahman'dur and his soaring ambitions to conquer the Plenn Archipelagos, this was the sorry demise of his plans.

"Save me" came a mournful plea. Durril spun and faced the petitioner. A ghost so tenuous he could hardly see it appeared when he used a well-cast observation spell. It held out lacy tendrils of ectoplasm so pale they vanished in the sunlight. Spots where eyes had been in life glowed a pale green.

"Why should I do anything of the sort?" asked Durril. "I exorcise spirits such as you."

"Please. The pain. It is cold here, and the pain! I cannot stand an instant more." The ghost fluttered around, almost tearing apart as hot wind gusted forth from the canyon. "Yet I must. I am trapped, doomed!"

Durril took pity on the poor specter. It had never asked to be enlisted in Rahman'dur's wild scheme of conquest.

"What were you in life?"

"A farmer. I raised soybeans and pin sprouts. I died. Rahman'dur killed me during the Spell Wars, and Lord Zoranto cursed me. My shade walked the island until Rahman'dur bound me to his accursed legion."

"You do not wish to feel this pain any longer?" Durril was intrigued by the conversation. For all his years of experience with exorcism, he had never carried on as lengthy a conversation with a spirit as he did now with this one.

"Cold, pain, it's all terrible. And memories! I remember living! That is the worst!"

Durril waved his hands and cast an appropriate exorcism spell. The farmer's ghost shrieked in pain then began to separate. Through the observation spell, he watched it grow and grow, becoming so thin that a bird flew through the substance and never noticed. The ghost expanded further and then disappeared for all time.

"Rest easy," Durril wished his unnamed victim.

He stared for a moment at the clean, clear blue sky. Rahman'dur had perverted magic by creating ghosts where none had been before. The plight of those trapped between life and death was solemn and sad enough. To intentionally create such beings was worse than wrong, it was immoral.

The rumblings from the valley sent shockwaves through the ground. The valley floor sank in response. The city sucked in much of the land; he wondered where the rest went. Staying to find out meant only death.

Scrambling up the hill gave him some protection. When debris and bits of sharp rock began to fly from the earthquake, he bent his head and rushed upward as fast as he could. He got to the first narrow ledge just as it began to crack and tumble back into the Valley of the Ultimate Demise.

It became difficult but not impossible to reach the upper ledge. The quake and rising dust cloud obscured everything below. He knew the giants had perished in the landslides—at least, he hoped they had. To have stayed to witness firsthand their demise would have been folly in the extreme.

"Not that I'm not a giddy fool for all I've done this day," he said to himself.

He set out, whistling off-key and content that he had done all mankind a service, though none would appreciate it and only a few would know.

"You! You've returned to watch him die. I wondered if you had the balls for it, I did, I truly did." The old scavenger still perched atop a rock like a human vulture waiting for its dinner to die.

"Nay," said Durril. "It's not to watch him die that I've come back." He pulled the locket from his tunic and dangled it in the sunlight. As it turned slowly, it cast bright reflections in all directions. The grizzled scavenger watched it as if it were his next meal.

Durril did not want to ask.

"What have you done with the armor and weapons from Lord Northdell's men?"

"Sold, each and every piece. And your amulet worked right good, she did, she really did." The scavenger cackled like a hen. "Can't wait to get more money and see if it'll keep on working."

"For your lifetime, it will work," Durril promised him, lying and knowing it. The amulet against social diseases would weaken over the days and months—true magical creations required constant work to maintain. Rahman'dur had built a magical generator to sustain his constructs. For years, it had worked well. When the generator vanished because of Durril's clever spells, they slipped permanently into the physical world. The magic in the cheap periapt he had given the old man would soon fade, leaving only a tacky piece of gold-plated base metal on a chain and fine memories.

By then Durril—and Arpad Zen—would be far away from Loke-Bor.

"You can have the locket when I'm finished with it," he promised. "You deserve something for watching over Arpad."

"For all the good the watching has been," the old man said, shaking his balding white-haired head. "He's damned near gone, he is."

Durril hastened to his apprentice and saw the truth in the old man's statement. Zen lay on his back, sightless eyes staring at the blue sky. Durril swiped his hand above those eyes and watched for response. The pupils dilated then contracted slightly. A hand held in front of Zen's nose detected only faint breathing. Other than this, he got no response from the supine man.

"He's far gone, is he not?" demanded the scavenger. "Did I do right to take what's on him?"

"He'll recover," Durril made sure he sounded more confident than he felt. He popped open the locket and let one grain of the powder within the stricken man's nose.

Nothing happened. He tried a second grain...and a third...and a fourth. Only when he had completely emptied the locket and began a strength spell did Zen respond. His eyelids fluttered, and a hint of color returned to his cheeks. Although still desperately ill and under the influence of the cerberus dog's poisonous blood, Arpad Zen would live.

Durril continued to work for that end, and hours later actually began to believe.

"He's sleeping now, is he?"

"Yes," Durril said, exhausted from his vigil. He had given Zen as much of his strength through conjuring as he dared.

"Then he might be wanting these back." The old scavenger dropped a bag of booty beside the sleeping man.

Durril searched through the pile and took out the apprentice's grimoire and magical implements. The rest, along with the locket, he handed back to the scavenger, who silently accepted them. The old man bobbed his head, spat in the direction of Rahman'dur's valley and scuttled from sight.

Durril leaned back against a rock, eyes closed and body weary beyond belief. He felt the quakes still wracking the valley, but his apprentice's smooth, even breathing and returning color made up for all the destruction he had wrought.

The spotted dog strolled up and stared at him, then dropped flat and laid its mangy head on crossed paws.

Chapter 16

"They just left me?" Arpad Zen cried in outrage.

"That they did, that they did," said the old scavenger. "If it wasn't for your friend here, and me, too, of course, you'd be a dead one now. Not even a ghost to wander around moanin' and groanin', no, sir. That magic dog blood is vicious stuff. Binds you up, it does."

"It also stopped up my nose," said Zen.

"You're well enough to get back to Castle Northdell. We've got wages to collect from the lord and his new lady."

Durril tried to keep the disappointment from his voice and failed. Zen noticed it immediately.

"It was a fool's errand, master. Look at the problems the pair of them caused. Lord Northdell lost an army, and Lady Kalindi..." His voice trailed off when he saw his master did not want to hear about unrequited love, especially from an apprentice.

"You get on back there and tell that fancy-ass lord to help out the poor folks of the countryside," said the old man. "I've got nothing to scavenge for a living now that you upped and killed Rahman'dur. The amulet won't do me diddly-good if I don't have money to spend."

"We'll tell him," promised Durril.

He put his arm around Zen's shoulders and heaved. The apprentice had taken a few days to recuperate and found his feet quickly. Walking proved difficult, but they kept the pace slow, and he strengthened from the exercise.

"The dog is following us," remarked Durril after a trio of hours on the trail. He wished that their horses had been available, but the animals had run off during the earthquake that devastated Rahman'dur's constructs.

"Dog?" Zen turned to see the small spotted dog trotting along a dozen yards behind. The animal studied them as they proceeded. The apprentice shrugged it off. "He's just looking for a free meal. You'll find none here, cur!"

He started to throw a rock, but Durril stopped him.

"It never pays to make an enemy."

"We might need such a fine animal for dinner one night," Zen said, loud enough for the dog to overhear.

The dog stopped and cocked its head, as if trying to decide if Zen was serious. It yelped once and resumed its position as they continued. By the end of the day, neither wizard nor apprentice noticed that the dog capered beside them. It had become a part of their trip.

◆

"Ahoy, Castle Northdell!" cried Durril, using a spell to deepen his voice slightly and make the words reverberate. The soldiers on the battlements responded immediately.

"The main gates remain open. Lord Northdell fears nothing," said Zen. "And why should he? We drove away most of the ghosts before killing Rahman'dur."

The dog barked loudly, as if disputing the point.

"The ogre," Durril said. "The ogre returned to the castle after kidnaping Kalindi."

His smile broadened. He had expected trouble when they returned. Now the agreed payment—and more!—would be theirs. When a lord had trouble, he needed help. If all had been well within the castle, they would have been shut out and sent on their way.

"Here he comes," said Zen. "The lord of the manor himself."

Lord Northdell rode forth on a white charger. His demeanor had changed greatly from the cringing poltroon. He sat erect in the saddle and a slight sneer curled his lips. His sandy hair blew as he rode.

"You, wizard. There is work to do in the castle."

"The ogre?" Durril took some delight in letting the word roll off his tongue and drive into the young lord's heart. A flash of fear passed like a storm cloud over Lord Northdell's face.

"What else? You neglected to destroy him as you did the others."

"There might be a few poltergeists remaining, too," guessed Zen. "They used to be my specialty—until I was abandoned and a desolate old man had to care for me."

Zen's jibe had no effect on Lord Northdell. He stared boldly at Durril, his blue eyes blazing.

"We had an agreement, wizard. You have not completed it."

"Prepare the ship and the trade goods—ones suitable for the lovely port of Wonne. We will turn out the ogre in a few hours. First, however, Arpad requires food and rest."

"In the kitchens. Go there, and the servants will give you what you need. I must hurry. I am late for my afternoon ride with Lady Kalindi."

"We'd hate for you to miss a single exhilarating moment of that," said Zen.

Durril cast him a sharp look. The apprentice fell silent. There was still a hint of feeling in his master for the lovely, vain lady.

They watched Lord Northdell ride away before saying anything more. Durril told his apprentice, "We do not need to hurry. We can recuperate first. I need rest. You need both rest and food."

"Relaxation would be appreciated," said Zen.

"Leave the kitchen wenches alone. You're lucky to be alive. The cerberus dog's blood damaged much."

"I need to find out how much, don't I?" Zen suggested.

"No."

"Yes, master," he said contritely. He had experienced a rush of power when confronting Lord Northdell so boldly. Durril put him in his place. An apprentice obeyed his master. It was that simple.

They went to the kitchen and found the staff uncooperative. Before, they had been frightened but willing to aid them. Now, no one cared.

"A change in policy works miracles," Durril commented dryly.

"A lord commands. He need not have his peasants like him if they obey. Lord Northdell is not a likable sort any longer, not that I found him such before. How he treats his vassals is none of our concern."

"In the strictest sense, you are right," admitted Durril. "There should be more to ruling, though, than being a dictator."

They wandered through the kitchen, finding scraps of food that had not spoiled overmuch. Durril took a haunch of meat and jumped onto a counter to eat. Zen sought out food more suitable for his needs. His belly complained constantly, and the type of food he put in it seemed important. After he found some beet soup and a loaf of bread without too much mold on it, he lost himself in eating. He wolfed down the tiniest morsels then worked up to more substantial portions.

"Don't be such a pig," came a high, shrill voice.

"I won't, master." Arpad stopped and looked up. Durril sat at a table drinking thin soup from a bowl. He shook himself. He hadn't heard anyone speak. It had been a hallucination. He resumed eating.

"Your belly will explode. Then where will you be?"

Zen's left hand flashed to his belt. His sword was gone, taken by Durril. He worked his fingers back farther and found a tiny ring. He pulled. A slender-bladed knife whistled into view.

"Show yourself, knave."

"I am."

He uttered a small observation spell to reveal the ghost haunting him. On the far side of the kitchen appeared a weak poltergeist, but the remnant was too fragile to even fully manifest. Speaking would lie far beyond its feeble power.

He saw no one else.

Durril wiped the soup from his lips and leaned back, his eyelids lowering as sleep overtook him.

"Master?"

"Let him sleep. He's worked hard on your behalf. You treat him too familiarly, if you ask me. You should be a better apprentice."

Zen jumped to stand, dropping into a fighting stance. "Come out and fight me!"

"I am out. Rather, I am in. I hate being put out, if you catch the pun." A tiny yelp followed.

Startled, Zen looked down at the spotted dog that had followed them from the Valley of the Ultimate Demise. The dog sat on its haunches, eyes fixed intently on him.

"You talk!"

"No jokes, please. I try not to let many people know. They take it the wrong way. The idea I might tell someone about the things I smell strikes many humans as outrageous—and sufficient reason to kill me." The dog turned one skinny haunch around and showed Zen a scar. "See? A man cheating on his wife did that after I saw him and his best friend's wife in the hay together."

"What did he do?" Zen asked, curious in spite of his skepticism that this was a prank Durril played on him.

"I told him his wife had already cuckolded him with the woman's husband. He threw a pitchfork at me. One tine cut a tendon. I still drag that leg slightly."

"This is a rich jape, master," Zen said, looking from the dog to the sleeping Durril. "How do you control your voice so perfectly? It seems as if the dog actually speaks."

"I do, fool."

"I need take no more insults," Zen said angrily. He motioned, his hand weaving bright green trails in the air as his spell formed. The dog howled and tried to run. Zen stopped it with a minor paralysis spell, then finished his major conjuring.

A ball of green, glowing energy darted from his fingertip to explode in front of the dog. The animal screeched and rose on its hind legs, then fell over.

Zen hadn't intended to kill it. The spell had been meant to frighten and nothing more, but the dog lay unmoving on the kitchen floor.

Durril stirred, his eyes fluttering open. Zen went closer to examine the dog. A mist rose from the animal and then turned into wispy columns of faint pink fog.

"It was possessed," marveled Zen.

"What?" Durril exploded from his chair when he saw the pink vapor drifting toward the door. As he rushed outside, he cast spell after spell. Zen stood in open-mouthed disbelief. He had seldom seen his master this agitated.

The apprentice followed his master and the turbulent pink fog outside. From high above came a shrill screech. Zen ducked back into the kitchen—he knew the sound of a hunting falcon when he heard it.

The bird plummeted from the sky, its pinions cracking with the force of its descent. To his surprise, it flapped frantically and landed on Durril's wrist as if trained from the egg for this post. The pink vapor narrowed and intensified in color, then rushed forward and entered the bird's open beak. The heavy bird of prey shuddered; Durril steadied it on his wrist. After it regained strength and sidestepped up and down his arm, he turned to Zen.

"That was a cruel and foolish thing to do."

"What? I only meant to give the dog a burn on its nose. I thought you—" Cold enveloped Arpad Zen when he realized his master had not been playing a trick on him.

"It's a familiar. As such, it can be useful to us."

"A familiar?"

"My name is Morasha," the bird said. "That dunderpate of an apprentice killed me!"

"It's all right now," soothed Durril. "This body is serviceable."

"It is strong. And I've always fancied the notion of flight." The bird stretched its long wings and flapped a few times. "Yes, I do like this body, Master Durril."

Morasha turned a gimlet eye on Zen and said, "You're no better than the farmer who pitchforked me. Worse. He didn't kill me."

"I never meant..." Zen shook his head, words failing him.

"You were never meant to think, that much is certain. I heard you earlier boasting of all the ghosts driven from this castle." The bird spat.

"They're not?" Arpad Zen stared at Morasha as if he had never seen a falcon before.

"The ogre is now a completely physical being," Morasha said. "As the others became solid and lost their ectoplasmic link, so did the ogre. Durril killed the other constructs. How will you slay the ogre, simpleton?"

"How will we?" Zen asked.

To that, he received no answer from his master. Morasha screeched loudly and sat on Durril's arm, looking smug.

Chapter 17

Durril stroked the sleek feathers along the hunting falcon's head. The wicked beak opened and closed gently on the wizard's index finger in a gesture of affection.

"You are good to me, Master Durril," the bird said. "This is a fine body." Wings beat at the air and launched the familiar high into the sky. Within seconds, only a brown dot remained. Then the bird vanished completely.

"I've never heard of such beings," said Arpad. "Are they useful?"

"They are, unless you anger them." Durril frowned and began to pace. "Morasha said the ogre has lost its link to the spirit world and now completely inhabits the physical."

"So?" Arpad Zen stared after Morasha, still unsure. His master had a strange sense of humor. This might be an elaborate prank, though he was coming slowly to believe the truth of what Durril—and Morasha—had said.

"I'll discuss the matter with Lord Northdell when he returns from his ride." Bitterness tinged the wizard's voice. Zen shook his head. It was beyond belief that his master still cared one whit for Kalindi, yet this seemed to be the case.

Durril went back into the kitchen, leaving his apprentice outside in the courtyard. Zen flinched and stepped back when he heard a falcon's hunting cry. Before he saw the bird, wings beat at his face and head. He threw out his arm to protect himself and felt powerful claws squeeze down.

"Quit flailing about so much, fool," came Morasha's order. "You'll dislodge me. And you would not like the consequences, I assure you!"

Zen stared at the heavy bird perched on his forearm. One yellow eye glared at him.

"You've followed us for some time. Why?"

"It's not illegal."

"It might be immoral."

The bird sneezed and shook its head. With a neck twist impossible in other creatures, Morasha turned and began preening.

"It amazes me how quickly I adapt to each new body. All the proper responses are inbred."

"You did not answer my question," said Zen.

"That's no crime, not answering your questions. Who are you to interrogate me?"

"I don't even know who you are. Durril claims you are a familiar."

"See? I said you spoke too informally of your master. You do it again." Morasha clucked, more like a hen than a falcon, and returned to the task of grooming.

Zen took a deep breath and considered smashing the irritating creature against the castle's stone wall. His muscles tensed enough to cause Morasha to abandon her quest for good grooming and once more give him the eye.

"I'm quicker than you," she warned. "In this body, I can pluck out your eyes before you can get a good swing started."

"I mean you no harm."

"You killed me!"

"That was an accident. I meant only to frighten you away."

"It worked," Morasha said sullenly.

"What do you mean that the ogre is still within the castle and now a material being?"

Morasha sneezed and shook her head from side to side. "Why must I repeat myself for your feeble intellect? Your master knows. When Rahman'dur died, his constructs lost their ectoplasm."

"He maintained their ghostly nature with spells?"

"Of course, he did. Some were conjured. Those simply vanished, as a real ghost would. The others, the ones he infused with ectoplasm to make them invulnerable to mortal attack, those reverted." Morasha sneezed again. "I am allergic to you. I never sneezed this much when in the dog's body."

"You might be allergic to your own feathers," Zen said with a certain glee. He hoped it was true. Morasha would find herself sneezing constantly in this form.

"Your master killed the other constructs left behind by Rahman'dur. Of all his creations, only this castle's ogre remains." Another sneeze shook the powerful falcon body. "This single construct will prove your undoing, though. It is a dreadful creature. Mere magic will not daunt it."

"Impossible. If it has become a physical being, even as we are, it can be stopped magically. Just like that!" Arpad Zen snapped his fingers. Morasha sidestepped to clamp down forcefully on his forearm. He tried to snap his fingers again and couldn't.

"You speak out of turn. The ogre is powerful."

"My magic is more powerful."

Morasha turned her head away in disdain for such braggadocio.

"I'll show you. I'll find the ogre and dispatch him." Zen tensed to snap his fingers, but the talons prevented it. He snapped the fingers on his right hand, but the resulting noise was weak and insignificant. This angered him even more.

"Begone!" he ordered. "I'll get rid of the ogre and still have time to finish my meal."

"Don't," warned Morasha.

"Are you frightened of the ogre? You, in your fine falcon's body?"

Morasha sidestepped up and down Zen's left arm again. "I will accompany you on this fool's mission, if only to accurately report your death to Durril."

Zen laughed and stalked off. Morasha flapped her wings and landed on his shoulder, claws cutting into his flesh. Zen said nothing. He settled his mind and tried to ignore the pain from those steely talons. Spells of lesser and greater potency flashed through his mind. He had yet to recover fully from his ordeal in the Valley of the Ultimate Demise, but he felt up to the task of ridding Castle Northdell of the ogre.

Hadn't Morasha claimed it had lost all ectoplasmic protection? He had not even meant to kill the dog body she had inhabited. The spell he had cast had been small, simple, hardly worth mentioning. By creating a major spell of the same order and type, he could snuff out the ogre's life-flame and never work up a sweat.

What physical beast could stand for even an instant against a wizard's apprentice of such great ability as himself?

"You track the ogre unerringly," commented Morasha. "You use a spell."

"An observation spell," Zen corrected. "It makes ghosts visible. The ogre retains enough magical charge to be visible to the spell."

"Does this not suggest difficulty in slaying the ogre?"

"You seek my humiliation with such words," snapped Zen, angry now. "You want me to turn and flee like a craven."

"Why?"

"I killed you accidentally."

"To be sure, but I still bear you no real malice. Return now, and fetch your master. Let him deal with the ogre."

"I'll finish the job we were engaged to do."

Zen went deeper into the unused north wing of the castle. His footsteps echoed eerily, and dust rose. He studied the stone floor to see if any had walked these corridors before him. He saw no disturbance in the dust, yet his magical sense told him the ogre waited ahead.

"Did the creature fly?" he wondered aloud.

"The ogre is cunning. It might have found other passages within the castle. These old places are filled with secret ways."

Zen stopped, the hair on the back of his neck standing. He turned slowly to face the ogre. The beast had seemingly emerged from a solid wall to stand behind him, blocking any possible retreat.

"Good. We no longer have to hunt you down," the wizard's apprentice said, with more bravado than he felt. His guts churned and sweat beaded his lip. He tried not to show panic. Any weakness now would mean his death.

A spell came to his lips. A tiny one, to be sure, but a spell that would serve him well. He summoned his master.

The ogre roared and raised powerful, hairy arms thicker than Zen's thighs. Clutched in one meaty hand was a heavy club. In the other swung a length of chain.

The chain sang and tangled Zen's legs. A quick tug brought him to the floor. He quickly cast a paralyzing spell, but the ogre simply shook himself like a wet dog and raised the club high for a killing blow.

Zen tried a more deadly spell—the most dangerous one he could conjure. The air boiled, and a lightning bolt sizzled toward the ogre's broad chest. The spell failed to stop the creature. Its chest hair ignited and burned with a greasy odor that clogged the nostrils, but other than this, the spell failed totally.

The only consolation he had was that the ogre had not turned it back on him as he did the night of Lord Northdell's ball.

Arpad Zen struggled to get his feet free of the chain and wiggle away. He failed, just as his most potent spell had.

The club sang through the air on an intersecting path with his head. Only Morasha's sudden flight down the hall, talons ripping and beak tearing, saved him. The club crashed off-target and destroyed part of the flagstone flooring.

Zen tried his spell again. Again it failed. No matter the type of spell he cast, the ogre shrugged it off. Roaring like a wounded bull, it thrashed around with its club in a vain attempt to stop Morasha's savage attack.

"Run, you fool," the bird cried. "Get away. I cannot hold him overlong."

Even as the words came from the hooked beak, the ogre changed tactics and stopped trying to hit Morasha with the club. Both hands grabbed for the bird.

The ogre bellowed in triumph as his powerful hands caught the falcon and began to squeeze. Blood and feathers erupted into the air, and Morasha went limp in the ogre's lethal grasp.

Zen watched in helpless horror as the ogre cast aside Morasha's carcass and turned its attention back to him. Bloody hands reached out for him. The apprentice tried not to panic and forget all his master had taught. He kept a steady flow of spells going, even though each took more strength than the last. Weakness spread like warm butter throughout his body.

Zen backed away from the ogre, seeking an escape route and not finding it. The creature had trapped him at the end of a long corridor. The doors leading off were barred from the inside. He tried not to think what that might mean. Of windows, he saw none.

"Better to die with an arrow in the forehead than one in the back," he said softly, remembering what his master always told him. He faced the ogre and prepared to die.

The ogre grabbed for him and missed. Zen danced to one side just as the ogre straightened and vented a howl of anger and pain. The beast slapped at something behind it.

"Master!" cried Zen. "My spells don't work!"

"It'll have to be killed with a sword," came Durril's voice.

The master wizard slashed at the ogre's legs and tried to cut the creature down to size. He missed and only pinked the monster on the thigh. A thousand cuts of that severity would be required to kill it.

"Why? Can't you cast a spell?"

"No." Durril began to pant as he worked to lunge and stay free of the ogre's clutching hands. "Some protection remains. I don't know if Rahman'dur intended it or not, but this one is the most powerful of all his constructs."

Durril slashed for the eyes, the sword tip finding the ogre's cheek. The brute reared back and touched the wound.

"The sharpening spell works well against it. All I have to do is get close enough for a killing thrust," gasped out Durril.

The wizard never got the chance to put his theory to the test. The ogre batted the sword blade away and rushed past Durril, going back to the spot in the hall-way where it had appeared behind Arpad Zen. It vanished into solid wall.

"A secret passage," said Durril. "Rooting it out from there will be even more dangerous." He bent forward, hands on knees until he regained his breath. He retrieved his fallen sword and asked, "What made you tread such a demented route?"

"Morasha." Zen's eyes widened. "The ogre killed Morasha!"

The apprentice rushed to the pile of broken bones and feathers and gingerly lifted the head. One yellow eye glared at him, accusing him of again being the agent for her death.

Chapter 18

"She's dying!" cried Arpad Zen. Pink vapor clung like morning mist around the falcon's body. The eye blinked once, then opened, glazing with death.

"Find another body. Be quick about it!" snapped Durril. He grabbed the falcon and cradled it as he might a baby. Zen raced into the courtyard. Durril followed more slowly, his lips already working on the complex spell that would insure a safe and painless transposition from one body to another for Morasha.

"Here, master. I found a—"

"Enough! Silence!" Durril closed his eyes and let the magical power well up within. The spell was not one he cast often.

The familiar's liberated spirit rose from the falcon's cooling body in a misty spiral of pink motes, then formed into an arrow heading directly for the creature Zen had found. Durril sank to his knees, exhausted from the strain of combat with the ogre and the casting of such a complicated spell. His eyes shot open when he heard the scream of anguish.

"Nooo! You cannot do this to me!"

Durril fought down a moment of hysterical laughter. Settling his mind and gaining control once more over himself, he said, "Arpad, is that the best you could do?"

His apprentice held a wiggling, angry piglet. Morasha's new body was covered with slop, and the tiny corkscrew tail worked frantically, as if trying to unwind.

"I'm sorry, master. I couldn't find anything else in time."

"Time was important," agreed Durril.

"The fool put me into a pig's body!" shrieked Morasha. "Do you take only simpletons for apprentices?"

"This isn't as fine a home as the falcon, that I grant you," Durril said. "But we had little chance to find anything more suitable. Would you prefer complete dissolution?"

"No!" The frantic tone in Morasha's voice convinced Durril she meant to live on, no matter the worldly form.

"We'll see about finding a body befitting a familiar of your stature when we have a spare moment," Zen assured her.

"Fool. Dunce. Cretin!"

"Now, now, don't go on like that. It isn't polite." Zen held the squealing piglet at arm's length. "Would you prefer a return to the wallow?"

"I'd prefer a decent body. This is humiliating! How could you do this to me after I saved your life?"

Zen's amusement at the familiar's fate died. She *had* saved him from the ogre.

"It's true, master," he said. "The ogre outwitted me and would have slain me."

"It's a force to be reckoned with," agreed Morasha.

"Quiet." Durril motioned both familiar and apprentice to silence as Lord Northdell rode into the courtyard at a trot, Kalindi at his side. The woman's platinum-white hair shone in the warm sunlight like burnished metal. She smiled, and it was just for Durril. His heart raced faster as he bowed in their direction.

"Lord, Lady," he greeted.

"You're still here?" Lord Northdell's attitude was one of complete scorn.

"We remain because the ogre remains. We contracted to remove all the spirits, and although the ogre has become entirely physical, we are honorbound to drive it from your home."

"Yes, yes, do so immediately. Quit wasting my time."

"Lord, one moment, please," said Durril, holding down his rising ire. "You mistake my position within these walls."

"Do I?" Lord Northdell sneered. "You are in my employ—my *employ*. I am lord of Loke-Bor, and you are under my command."

Durril looked from the arrogant young lord to Kalindi. Her bright eyes locked with his, then broke away when Lord Northdell jerked on her horse's reins. She cast a final, pleading glance in Durril's direction, then sat stolidly in the saddle, back rigid and staring ahead.

"Let's leave the ogre," said Zen. "Such effrontery I have never seen! How dare he talk to you like that?"

"We will fulfill the terms of the agreement as I see

them, Arpad. Perhaps he acts in this manner to impress Lady Kalindi."

"I remember him soiling his fine garments as fear clawed at his gut. We drove away the spirits haunting his fine palace. Has he forgotten so easily?"

"Has he forgotten also how he led his troops into the jaws of a trap? Their spirits might have roamed the Valley of the Ultimate Demise forever if you had not killed Rahman'dur," pointed out Morasha.

"Rahman'dur would have put that young pup in the ground, too," said Zen.

"Enough. We've got to find the ogre and dispatch him. Tell me all you can remember of your encounter." Durril cleared his throat and glared at his apprentice. "Start with your reasoning for tackling such a creature without my assistance."

Zen and Morasha alternated describing the encounter. Durril made them repeat several parts. Morasha finished, saying, "The ogre is Rahman'dur's most effective conjuring. As Arpad learned, spells alone will not kill it."

"Nor, as I learned, will steel alone slay the monster. We must combine the two modes of attack if we are to succeed," said Durril, lost in thought.

"How, master? I can barely lift my arms. Weakness floods over me like our Mother Ocean."

"Weakness flows *from* you, too," said Morasha. "Snivel and whine any more, and I'll have nothing more to do with this mad scheme."

"Be quiet, or I'll serve you for dinner. Pork chops are a favorite of mine."

"Cannibal!"

Durril looked up, barely aware of their bickering. "Both spell and sword," he said, sure of his decision.

"You cannot swing the sword, Arpad, so I must. You'll have to cast the spell."

"I am weak, master."

"Is the ogre in better shape? We fought it individually. Now, we must combine," said Morasha.

"She is accurate in her appraisal of the situation," said Durril.

"A piglet? What good can she be to us?" scoffed Zen.

Morasha tried to bite him.

"Never turn away from an ally," said Durril. "What she lacks in strength and size, she makes up for in cunning. Is that not so, familiar?"

"Naturally, it is, Master Durril."

The wizard checked his sword. The left-handed grip still felt awkward to him, but his destiny with the steel blade lay clear and sharp before him. Zen would cast the spell, he would drive the sword through the ogre's vile heart. He began the sharpening spell that had proven so effective against Rahman'dur's other constructs.

"Now," he said. "We go now. If we wait any longer, we stalk the ogre in darkness."

"The castle corridors are dimly lit," said Morasha. "Would a torch improve our chances?"

"Doubtful," said Durril. "The scent would alert the ogre to our presence. Even a hint of surprise on our side might mean the difference between life and death."

"Let's get Lord Northdell to furnish a squad of soldiers. We can use their strong arms and—" Zen bit back his words when he saw the way both his master and the pig glared at him. "I'm sorry, master. We agreed to remove the spirits, and we have to finish the chore."

"Some hint of honor is being driven into him, I see," said Morasha. "How you work with such tarnished metal, however, is beyond me. Truly, Durril, you must be a wizard of the first order. Besides, Northdell doesn't have a squad of soldiers left after the debacle leading his army against Rhaman'dur."

Zen kicked at the pig and missed, almost falling. Durril grabbed his apprentice's collar and pulled him along.

"Enough bickering. Listen carefully. This is the most important spell you can learn." Durril began drilling his pupil in the complex killing spell.

"The ogre turned it on you, master. Remember?"

Durril shuddered. The blackness of the lightning bolt that had come back at him on the balcony still sucked at his very soul. Only chance had allowed him to avoid Rahman'dur's creature's potent counter-thrust.

"That was a product of Rahman'dur's skill and the ogre's partially ectoplasmic existence. Both are passed. We must add the ogre to this list."

Durril's arms and legs moved as if dipped in lead. His head ached, and his breathing came in ragged gusts. A month's rest might put him right. He had done too much and received too little recognition for it. Lord Northdell should have hailed him as a hero after killing Rahman'dur. The late wizard had intended to spread his magical hold over Loke-Bor until he controlled the entire Plenn Archipelagos. Instead of rewarding Durril for preventing this, Lord Northdell had reviled him.

Durril knew the reason. Lord Northdell was new to power, and it corrupted him. Coldness spread in his gut when he realized jealousy also played a part in the lord's attitude. A blinded fool couldn't miss the passion between wizard and lady.

A squeal brought him out of his reverie. Morasha rushed to the door leading back into the deserted wing of the sprawling castle. She edged open the door with her snout and raced ahead.

"Morasha! Come back!" Durril cursed under his breath. He knew what she intended, and it did not mesh well with his own plans. She risked her own life to decoy the ogre into the open.

"After her!" cried Zen. "She'll be killed again. No one, not even her, should die three times in a single afternoon."

Durril smiled crookedly. His apprentice felt some compassion toward the strange spirit they had found—or who had found them. Arpad still felt a tinge of guilt over accidentally spell-killing the dog. And Morasha had saved him from the ogre. Durril had seen enough of the fight to realize that.

"There!" cried Zen. "The ogre is following her. It worked. Morasha lured him out of hiding!"

Durril ran after his apprentice, worried at the ease of the ploy. The ogre had emerged, not from a hidden passageway but from solid stone wall. Some vestige of magic lingered in the lumbering monstrosity's makeup. Durril knew that ridding Castle Northdell of its hairy presence would be vastly more difficult than he had feared.

"Arpad, duck!" he yelled.

His apprentice sensed the danger and dived forward, sliding along the stone floor on his belly. Durril saw the bloody swath left where the skin peeled away from Zen's chest. The ogre bellowed in anger, having missed a chance to dispatch his enemy with ease. The brute raised its heavy club and swung. The blow missed Zen by a hand's breadth.

Durril wasted no time rushing to assist, but Morasha arrived before him. The piglet squealed and ran between the ogre's legs. The towering freak kicked hard and caught her in the side, but the action caused it to lose its balance. It fell to one knee.

The wizard called, "The spell, Arpad. Begin the spell!" He lunged, even though he was off-balance and too far away to deliver a fatal thrust. The tip of his blade slid along the ogre's upper arm and left a muddy track of inky black blood. The ogre rewarded him with a bellow of pain and a swing of the club.

Durril stumbled back as the club ripped past just under his nose. He felt the hot wind from the passage and knew he had missed having his head turned to bloody pulp only through luck.

Recovering, he assumed a better fighting stance. He heard Zen working on the exorcism spell. The air around the ogre's head boiled and churned from the force of the spell, but the creature shook off the effect.

"The aura!" called Zen. "I see it sucking away its very soul!"

"Not so," corrected Morasha. The piglet danced back and forth, squealing and trying to nip at the ogre's ankles. Even when she was successful, the beast paid her no heed. The injuries she inflicted were minor compared to its strength and vitality.

"The spell is turning the ogre's head green. Look!"

Durril held down his rising gorge. They were the ones trapped and in danger. The green miasma emanating from the ogre's head showed the power of the residual magics locked within it, not its vulnerability.

His nose wrinkled at the mounting stench. His hands shook, and his knees threatened to buckle under him. The ogre had been cut off from Rahman'dur's magic and had lost much of the protection given by its ectoplasm, but the emerald gas provided a deadly protection.

Durril quick-stepped forward and lunged, his blade sinking into the ogre's belly. He jerked to one side and opened a gash halfway across the hairy stomach. The ogre groaned but showed no weakening.

"Keep conjuring," he urged Zen. "We've got to wear it down." His heart sank when more green gas billowed forth in response to Zen's spell. Durril knew then he had chosen the wrong mode of attack, but it was too late to give his apprentice another spell. Holding his breath, he waded back in to the attack.

Morasha and he formed a well-coordinated fighting team. The pig could not damage the ogre, but she distracted it from time to time, giving Durril the opportunity to drive in his sword. The ogre accepted a prodigious amount of punishment and still fought like ten men.

The ogre brought its club up against the wizard's sword with a resounding crack. Durril sailed backwards, falling flat on his back. Morasha ran between the ogre's legs again, slowing the behemoth until Durril could regain his balance.

He faced the ogre armed only with his dagger.

"The spell!" he called. "Keep conjuring. Don't stop!" He heard Arpad mumbling. He started to warn him against changing the spell, then found himself embraced by brawny arms that lifted him off the floor with contemptuous ease.

Durril gasped as the air rushed from his lungs. Blackness closed in as the ogre applied pressure to his trapped arms and lower back.

"The dagger, Master Durril," came Morasha's voice, as if from the other side of the Plenn Archipelagos. "Twist it!"

Durril wiggled slightly in the ogre's grip and felt the handle of the dagger. He had driven it into the creature's ribs when the arms encircled him. With the last of his strength, he twisted the weapon.

The pressure on his back lessened.

Durril tried to follow through and shove the dagger into the ogre's vile heart, but all strength had fled his body. He fell to the floor, gasping for air.

Through a thin veil of black, he watched the battle continue. Morasha nipped at the monster's legs, and Arpad cast the spell.

It took Durril several seconds to understand what was happening.

"No, Arpad, don't change the spell!"

The debilitating green mist that had risen from the ogre gave the creature an edge in the fight, but it also sapped its ability to fight magic. If Arpad had maintained the spell, the gas would have vanished eventually, leaving the ogre susceptible to the devastating force of the incantation.

By changing the spell, Zen had allowed the ogre a brief respite.

Durril forced himself to his feet and dived forward. His arms enclosed the ogre's waist from behind, and he found the dagger hilt. He jerked it toward him, into the ogre, with all his remaining energy.

An inhuman screech of pain was his reward before being tossed hard against the corridor's stone wall.

Durril lost consciousness for a few seconds. The next thing of which he was aware was a rough, wet tongue working on his face. He blinked his fogged eyes and saw a pig snout.

"The ogre," Morasha cried. "We must find it!"

"Wh-What happened?" The world around him came into better focus as he sat up. He winced as cracked ribs began their protest. He tried to touch the injured spot and found that the palms of his hands had been stripped of flesh. Durril remembered his double-handed grip on the dagger handle. He had not wanted to release the dagger's rough handle, and the ogre had thrashed about to cause this new injury.

He only hoped that the monster had come out the loser in the battle.

"Where is it?" he asked, his voice strengthening.

"Ran away," gasped out Arpad Zen. "I'm sorry, master. I changed from the spell you taught me to another. The green gas...it was robbing me of my power."

Durril waved off the mistake. They were alive—and Arpad had learned this lesson.

"After it. We can still dispatch it." Holding back a moan of agony, he fetched the fallen sword, and the trio set off after the ogre, following a trail of tenebrous blood.

"It goes back to the balcony where we first saw it," said Zen.

"Where it kidnapped Kalindi," Durril said, his voice cold and resolve firming within him.

"There!" Morasha ran to the railing and thrust her pig snout through to see the hillside below. "The ogre flees like a craven!"

The ogre lurched away, clutching at its midsection. Durril tried to guess if the dagger wound would prove fatal soon. He failed. The ogre had shown too much stamina—and residual magic. Rahman'dur's death had robbed it of contact with the spirit world, but some of that ectoplasmic power and protection remained. Some, a little, enough? He had no idea.

"The ogre has been driven from the castle," the wizard said softly. "We have fulfilled our contract. Let's receive our reward for this odious task from Lord Northdell."

Barely able to walk, he went to find the lord of the castle—the completely exorcised castle.

Chapter 19

"The deed is done," said Durril. "The ogre has been driven from the castle."

Lord Northdell looked around nervously, then straightened as if courage flowed into him. His arm snaked out and circled Kalindi's waist. He pulled her close. Durril saw the expression of distaste on the woman's face.

"They are gone? All the spirits?"

Durril nodded, too weary to speak.

"But my advisers report that the ogre is not dead. You allowed it to escape into the forest."

"We drove it from your castle. It will not trouble you again."

"It will!" Something of the young lord's old fear returned. "It can come back when you leave. You must kill it. Kill it! You must! You promised!"

Durril knew tracking the ogre would be easy—its dark blood seared the ground wherever it touched, but he had no idea how dangerous the creature still was. He

187

resented having to deal further with Rahman'dur's creation yet saw the need. He had given his word to exorcise—to permanently remove—all the spirits within the castle. If the ogre lived on, even in physical form, he had not completed the contract.

"It will be done," he agreed.

He cast one fond look at Kalindi. The woman's white-blonde hair shone in the afternoon sunlight and rivaled the jewels woven into the golden strands of the pearl necklace she wore. He started to speak to her, but she turned away and left with her husband-to-be.

Durril sighed. Kalindi was so beautiful it made his heart ache—almost as much as the rest of his body. He went to the courtyard where Morasha and his apprentice argued over their respective roles in routing the ogre.

"We must track and kill it before Lord Northdell pays," he said.

Arpad Zen shifted nervously. "Can we? It eluded us before."

"Scared? Are you a craven as well as a fool and a poor excuse for a wizard's apprentice?" taunted Morasha.

"You're still angry about being trapped in a pig's body."

"And why shouldn't I be? You killed me twice in one day! The dog was merely adequate for me, but you had to rob me of a perfectly fine falcon's body."

"This body is more appropriate to your nature," countered Zen.

"Silence!" Durril wanted nothing more than to slay the ogre and be on his way to Wonne with a ship loaded to the gunwales with trade goods. This chore had taken on heroic proportions. Right now he felt anything but heroic.

"Sorry, master." Zen hung his head.

Morasha snorted and rooted about in the dirt.

"Your nose is appropriate for the tracking chores," Durril told Morasha. "Get on with it."

"The ogre's blood burns my nostrils," she complained.

"Pork chops are my favorite," whispered Zen.

Morasha snorted and began tracking, picking up ogre spoor just outside the castle walls. Durril followed slowly, his lips moving in the incantation needed to spell-sharpen the sword. When he finished, he taught Zen a new spell to use against the ogre. They had weakened it; now they must not waver before killing it.

☽

"How close are we?" Zen asked nervously when Morasha found larger drops of the burning black blood. The seared spots on the ground made it obvious to even a neophyte tracker that they neared their wounded and dangerous prey.

"I hear the ogre," cried Morasha.

Durril heaved a deep sigh. The battle would be vicious. The ogre would fight like...a wounded ogre.

"Into the thicket. It must not leave those thorn bushes alive," he said.

With Arpad Zen to his right and Morasha to his left, Durril advanced to engage the ogre in a life-or-death fight.

☽

Lord Northdell lounged in his throne, his face marred by the sneer on his lips. He lifted his right hand and snapped his fingers. A servant rushed up with a wine-filled goblet.

"No, idiot!" raged the young lord. He backhanded the servant, sending her to the base of the dais, wine spattering everywhere. "Get rid of that silly slut and find a decent servant," he ordered the captain of his guard.

Durril stood at the door to the audience chamber, silently watching the petulant display.

"You, wizard. Have you succeeded?"

Durril advanced with effort, concealing the pain every step gave him. He tried to breath in shallow gasps to keep from crying out. He stopped at the foot of the wine-soaked platform.

To Lord Northdell's left sat Kalindi. Durril had seen happier expressions on men condemned to execution. She fidgeted and worried at a piece of lace in her lap. Her bright blue eyes were rimmed with red and tears welled. A bruise on her cheek bore the shape of a hand—Lord Northdell's hand.

The exquisite pearl-and-jewel gold-braided necklace dangled around her swan-like throat and captured Durril's attention and imagination. He fantasized lovingly removing it and...

"Well?" demanded the ruler of Loke-Bor. "Is it dead?"

"The castle is exorcised," Durril said. "All specters are gone, and the ogre will never again return to this castle. We destroyed it in the forest."

"Good. You have done well. Now be off. I cannot have your kind on Loke-Bor. Not after the trouble I had getting rid of Rahman'dur. I will not be responsible for starting a new bout of the Spell Wars."

Durril's eyes narrowed. "I killed Rahman'dur. And we had a contract. You owe me a fully laden trade ship with goods suitable for exchange in Wonne."

"Oh, do I? Does anyone in this room, save this addlepated wizard, remember such an agreement? I don't." The ruler's eyes flashed with a hint of madness. "My father, Zoranto the Magnificent, said never to deal with wizards. There is no reason to violate his dictum, is there? Is there?" The last words came out in a scream that echoed throughout the audience hall.

Durril watched not Lord Northdell but his intended bride. Kalindi winced at this perfidy. Try as he might, though, Durril could not catch her eye. She looked at the lace in her lap and ran her fingers in endless circles around it.

"Are you reneging on our agreement? Is this the limit of the honor of the Lord of Loke-Bor?" shouted Arpad Zen from the rear of the audience chamber. "Are you totally lacking in integrity?"

"Arpad." Durril's voice sounded sharp and steeledged. "I conduct business, not you."

Chastened, Zen fell silent.

"Yes, wizard, you conduct the business. And it is at an end. You have one minute to get out of my sight and one further minute to leave Castle Northdell. Failing this, I will order my soldiers to cut off your heads." Lord Northdell leaned on the right arm of his throne and looked smug and self-satisfied. The mood passed quickly. Dark madness descended. "Where is my wine? Bring me wine, or I'll cut off the fingers of everyone in the kitchen!"

"Lord Northdell," Durril said softly, his voice penetrating the silence following the ruler's outburst, "you should honor our agreement. It is not wise to cheat me."

"Guards! Throw them out! Get rid of them immediately, or your heads will be on pikes outside the castle walls to greet the morning sun!"

Durril held up his hand. The soldiers hesitated, fearing a wizard's wrath. Instead, Durril said, "We leave peacefully."

Lord Northdell snorted in contempt.

"I will collect my due, however."

"Escort them to the front gates—and slam the gates behind them," ordered Lord Northdell.

Durril spun and left the audience chamber, head high and a faint smile on his lips. He had dealt with petty rulers before. He had even seen the instability in this young lord and had expected difficulty collecting his payment.

With Zen at his side, he sauntered through the gates. Behind he heard the taunts of the castle guards. With great dignity, he turned and said in a voice loud enough to be heard by both peasants and guards watching from the battlements, "Close the gates. We would not want this to be too easy."

The soldiers obeyed uneasily.

Durril motioned for Zen to set up their portable stage, which had already been tossed out of the castle courtyard. Tension mounted as the apprentice struggled with the low wooden platform. Durril impassively watched, his hands hidden in the folds of the sleek, shining robe he had donned.

When Zen finished, Durril mounted the stage and turned to gesture dramatically.

"Lord Northdell! You refuse to pay me for ridding your castle of its specters. I now return them!"

A pass of his arm caused a dozen small tornadoes to spring up. Within the raging pillars of dust formed faces, figures—vaporous beings reaching for the castle walls. A gasp went up from the assembled guards and peasants. Many cried out in fear.

Durril let the miniature storms smash against the stone walls. None carried a real specter; all were simple illusions meant to prepare the masses for the show to come.

"He returns them to our midst. He didn't exorcise them," came the worried howls from the castle walls. "He only hid them!"

"That which you fear the most is now returned to you," shouted Durril. He clapped his hands and produced a tower of flame. From the center of the leaping flames lumbered the ogre.

The creature bellowed and rushed forward, heavy club crashing against the castle gate. The second blow ripped free one brass hinge. The tenth blow brought the gate crashing down.

"What is the meaning of this?" cried a frightened Lord Northdell from the battlements. "You can't send the ogre back to torment me! You can't!"

"You failed to pay. I am only restoring your castle to its condition before I began work." Durril's statement was punctuated by a loud growl from the ogre. It began ripping the other castle gate from its hinges. Soldiers cowered from the towering hairy figure.

"Wait, stop! Stop the ogre!"

"Why?"

"I–I'll pay!"

"We never had a contract. You claimed as much."

"No, I made a mistake."

"You lied. You tried to cheat me." Durril pressed the young lord unmercifully.

"Yes, I did all that. Stop the ogre. Get rid of it!"

"Arpad," the wizard said softly. "Go fetch our smelly friend."

Zen smiled. He rushed into the castle courtyard and approached the raging ogre cautiously. "Come along, now. Don't make such a fuss. Please," he added when the ogre gnashed long fangs at him. This simple word calmed the monster. Like an obedient dog, it trotted after the apprentice.

Durril walked to the sundered gate and motioned for Lord Northdell to join him. "My fee has grown, due to increased overhead. It is difficult controlling an ogre for long," he said, looking significantly at the violent beast.

"The merchant ship is yours. Messengers will be dispatched immediately to have it loaded and readied for sailing."

"There is more."

"What? You cannot cheat me!"

"No one can cheat an honest man. I find it simple to cheat *you*," Durril said in disgust. "I wish for the Lady Kalindi to accompany me."

"She's to marry me in a month's time!" protested Lord Northdell. His eyes widened in fear when the ogre bellowed. "Perhaps she should see more of the Plenn Archipelagos, though. A sea journey might do her a world of good."

"Such as a trip to Wonne?" suggested Durril. "That is my destination."

"Yes, yes, take her. Just don't release the ogre."

Durril left the young lord in the courtyard and went directly to Kalindi's quarters. The woman stepped back from the door when he entered, hand going to cover her mouth.

"There's nothing to fear," Durril said. "I've come to take you away from him."

"The ogre?" she asked, her blue eyes wide with fright. "You actually summoned it?"

"I...did," Durril stepped forward and reached for her, his hand circling her slender neck. The necklace of radiant jewels and pearls came unfastened and dropped to the floor.

"Oh!" She bent to retrieve it. Durril gently held her upright.

"I'm so clumsy. Allow me." He hunkered over and stood, the necklace dangling from his fingers. "Permit me to place it where it belongs." He refastened it around her neck. "Now, prepare a bag. You are leaving with me."

"Lord Northdell?"

"His power is broken. Soon after I leave there will be a castle coup." Durril shrugged. "I have no idea who will lead it, but it ought to be successful. Who is completely loyal to him?"

"No one," Kalindi said earnestly. "How can I thank you for freeing me? He turned into such a fiend!"

"It happens. Zoranto never trained him to assume the throne, and he lacked the will and inner strength to overcome that."

"Go," she said breathlessly. "Wait for me outside while I pack. I'll join you in a few minutes."

"Very well."

He left and paced the corridor. After a few minutes, he went to a window overlooking the stables and saw the heavy-set commoner Uldorf helping Kalindi climb down from a low roof. She had left through the window in her room immediately after Durril left it, taking nothing with her. He watched the lovely woman ride off with her peasant lover, a small smile crinkling his lips.

He reached into the folds of his robe and drew out the necklace. He had cleverly replaced it with a fake he had conjured. In hours, the conjured one would return to woven hemp string.

Balancing the necklace in his hand, he understood why Rahman'dur had wanted the jewels. Power surged into him. A spell mirror constructed of such jewels would give power unheralded since the Spell Wars. Durril wondered if Kalindi knew where other such gems were to be found.

Rahman'dur had tried to force the information from her, just as he had tried to forcibly remove the gems from her neck. The magic reaction had prevented the latter; and as far as Kalindi's knowledge of more jewels, he doubted she knew—and did not really care. These would serve him nicely. He tucked the necklace away and strode out, whistling off-key.

Subterfuge always worked better than brute force, even when dealing with magic.

"Master, they are loading the ship as Lord Northdell ordered. He used mirror signals to get the job started." Arpad Zen pointed to a scrying spell shimmering in the air and showing every bit of cargo being loaded.

"Amazing, isn't it, Arpad, how quickly a man can find honor and pay his debts when given the proper goad?" Durril motioned to the ogre, who snarled and bared its fangs.

"Get out of here—and take that with you!" Lord Northdell fell to his knees and begged.

"Very well," said Durril. "You have no further need of the ogre, I see." The wizard walked over to the huge, hairy monster and laid his hands on the partially healed chest wound caused by his dagger. Using the newfound focusing power of Kalindi's jewels, he worked a recuperative spell. The ogre sighed as pain went away.

"We should hurry, master," murmured Zen, staring at his scrying spell. "A band of castle officers is muttering about revolt."

"We should leave," agreed Durril. Softly, to the ogre, he said, "Come along, Morasha."

The ogre growled. "You couldn't kill the ogre. No, you had to let me, in my pig body, try to do that for you."

"Dying three times in a day must be tiresome," said Zen. "Just be thankful the ogre was nearby."

"I stink."

"You improved on your stature, if not your odor," pointed out Durril. "Think of the respect you'll be afforded."

"You should have killed the ogre and left me in the pig," grumbled Morasha.

"Never mind. We have seas to sail and treasure to spend."

"What of Kalindi, master?"

Durril smiled more broadly. "I have taken her most precious possession. What more can I want?"

"But you weren't gone long enough—" started Zen.

Morasha grabbed him in a hairy hand and shook until he fell silent. Zen straightened his tunic and shrugged. He was a mere apprentice. He should know when to ask questions—and when to refrain.

Whistling, the wizard walked off briskly down the road to the harbor, Arpad Zen and Morasha in her ogre body following.

END

Author's Note

The strange eddies of the publishing world originally brought this, the first book of the After The Spell Wars trilogy, to the light of day as well as the second volume, *In the Sea Nymph's Lair* but not the final volume, *The Wizard's Spell Mirror*. It is with great pleasure that I can now say all three will see print from Zumaya Otherworlds.

ABOUT THE AUTHOR

ROBERT E. VARDEMAN is the author of nearly two hundred novels spanning many genres, but his favorites have always been science fiction and fantasy. Most notable series: The Cenotaph Road, Weapons of Chaos, Biowarriors, Masters of Space, The Jade Demons, The Accursed and Demon Crown. He also has coauthored nine titles in the Swords of Raemllyn series with Geo W. Proctor. After twenty years, the reprinting of the first of the Star Frontier series and initial publication of the final two titles, The Genetic Menace and The Black Nebula brings the entire trilogy to the readers—finally. Individual titles include *Dark Legacy* (1996, Harper); a Magic: The Gathering tie-in novel, *Hellheart* (2000) Warner) and the MechWarrior tie-in novel, *Ruins of Power* (2003, ROC). He wrote the original Star Trek novels *The Klingon Gambit* (1981, Simon & Schuster) and *Mutiny on the Enterprise* (1983, Simon & Schuster).

Short fiction has been published in magazines such

as *Twilight Zone Magazine* and many anthologies. Recent appearances include "The Power and the Glory" in Time Twisters (2007, DAW Books), "Purification" in *Invasion!* (2007, Black Library), "Tontine" in *Sword & Sorceress* #23 (2007, Norilana Books) and "Wreckers" in *Pirates of the Blue Kingdoms: Shades and Specters* (2007, Walkabout Publishing). Publication of "To Cat, A Thief" is slated for December 2008 in *Catopolis*, with "Jack and the Genetic Beanstalk" to follow soon after in *Terribly Twisted Tales*, both from DAW Books. Vardeman's short fiction collection, *Stories from Desert Bob's Reptile Ranch* (2008, Walkabout Publishing), contains 21 stories spanning the horror, humor, science fiction and fantasy fields.

Under his "Karl Lassiter" pen name, he has written eight epic western novels, including *White River Massacre* (2002) and *Sword and Drum* (2003), all from Pinnacle Books. A "Karl Lassiter" short story, "After Blackjack Dropped," in the anthology *Lost Trails* (2007) was also published by Pinnacle Books. His first YA western, *Drifter*, was published in February 2009 by Avalon Books.

Vardeman's Peter Thorne mystery series includes *The Screaming Knife* (1990, Avon), *The Resonance of Blood* (1992, Avon) and *Death Channels* (1993, Avon). The high-tech thriller *Death Fall* (1991, Onyx) gave an opportunity to use his technical degrees in physics and engineering as background. More recently, using the "Cliff Garnett" pen name, he published *TalonForce: Seafire* (2001, NAL).

Robert E Vardeman has served as vice-president of the Science Fiction Writers of America (SFWA) and also edited the organization's Forum. He is a member of the Western Writers of America (WWA) and the International Association of Media Tie-in Writers (IAMTW), serving as a judge for that organization's

2007 Scribe Award, and is also a member since its inception in 1979 of the informal group First Fridays, founded by mystery writer Tony Hillerman. For the past five years, he has worked on the editorial staff of four fantasy football magazines and until recently worked as editor on the bimonthly Albuquerque magazine, *For Your Family*. As a member of the Coalition for Excellence in Science Education, Vardeman served as consultant to the New Mexico State textbook advisory board in 2003.

More about Robert E. Vardeman's fiction can be found on his web sites: www.CenotaphRoad.com and http://www.KarlLassiter.com.

ABOUT THE ARTIST

BRAD W. FOSTER is an illustrator, cartoonist, writer, publisher, and whatever other labels he can use to get him through the door! He's won the Fan Artist Hugo a few times, picked up a Chesley award and turned a bit of self-publishing started more than twenty-five years ago into the Jabberwocky Graphix publishing empire. (Total number of employees: 2.)

His strange drawings and cartoons have appeared in over two thousand publications, half of those science fiction fanzines, where he draws just for the fun of it. On a more professional level, he has worked as an illustrator for various genre magazines and publishers, the better known among those being *Amazing Stories* and *Dragon*. In comics he had his own series some years back, *The Mechthings*, and he even got to play with the "big boys" of comics for a few years as the official "Big Background Artist" of Image Comic's *Shadowhawk*.

Known throughout the world (though most of the world doesn't know it yet) for his intricate pen-and-ink work, it is possible you've seen more of work in titles as varied as *Cat Fancy, Cavalier,* or *Highlights for Children.* Most recently he has completed covers for a couple of Yard Dog Press books, illustrations for magazines such as *Space & Time* and *Talebones,* illustrations for the first of Carole Nelson Douglas' Cozy Noir Press books on Midnight Louie, and has even managed to work a dragon into the official poster for the 2003 Tulsa Oktoberfest!

He spends huge sections of the year with his lovely wife Cindy showing and selling his artwork at festivals and conventions around the country. Check out his website at www.jabberwockygraphix.com for the latest news!

ANGELA WATERS' eclectic tastes in music and books have converged with her fascination with technology. Sleepless nights are filled with listening to hardcore rockers and playing out the tunes in colors that describe her vision of an author's words. Her muse is thrilled it finally has a place to cut loose.

Printed in Great Britain
by Amazon

51318693R00128